# MONTANA MAVERICKS

*Welcome to Big Sky Country, home of the Montana Mavericks! Where free-spirited men and women discover love on the range.*

## THE ANNIVERSARY GIFT

The mayor of Bronco and his wife have invited the whole town to help celebrate their thirtieth anniversary, but when the pearl necklace the mayor bought his wife goes missing at the party, it sets off a chain of events that brings together some of Bronco's most unexpected couples. Call it coincidence, call it fate—or call it what it is: the power of true love to win over the hardest cowboy hearts!

Dylan Sanchez can sell anything to anyone, but as a novice rancher, he may be in over his head. Luckily, Robin Abernathy sees right through his apparent self-assurance. The independent horsewoman is sure she can rescue Dylan's new venture from ruin. Saving herself from falling for the flirty salesman might be a much bigger hurdle...

Dear Reader,

When I was a young romantic with stars in my eyes and I read a story about a confirmed bachelor, it was so difficult for me to relate to the concept. Who *wouldn't* want to fall in love and get married?

And then twenty-one years ago, I met my then fiancé's uncle Tommy.

Now, Uncle Tommy is the definition of the term *fun uncle*. My sons even bought him a T-shirt that says FUNCLE. He's the life of the party and people naturally gravitate toward him...especially the ladies. He's also a very successful sales broker without giving off that stereotypical salesman vibe. Sure, someone out there will come along one day and capture Uncle Tommy's heart, but it'll definitely take the right woman.

In *Sweet-Talkin' Maverick*, salesman Dylan Sanchez reminded me so much of Uncle Tommy. He adores his family, yet also enjoys his role as the last single Sanchez sibling. His relatives, though, have a different plan and convince him to host a Valentine's Day–themed bakeoff.

Horsewoman and business owner Robin Abernathy is more comfortable outdoors on a ranch than she is inside a kitchen. But that doesn't stop her from entering the contest in an effort to spend more time with her crush. Will it be Robin's secret cookie recipe or her skills at ranching that will eventually capture Dylan's heart?

For more information on my other books, visit my website at christyjeffries.com, or chat with me on Twitter at @ChristyJeffries. You can also find me on Facebook (authorchristyjeffries) and Instagram (@christy_jeffries). I'd love to hear from you.

Enjoy,
*Christy Jeffries*

# SWEET-TALKIN'
# MAVERICK

## CHRISTY JEFFRIES

Special thanks and acknowledgment are given to
Christy Jeffries for her contribution to the
Montana Mavericks: The Anniversary Gift miniseries.

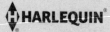

ISBN-13: 978-1-335-59474-7

Sweet-Talkin' Maverick

Copyright © 2024 by Harlequin Enterprises ULC

Recycling programs
for this product may
not exist in your area.

Harlequin Enterprises ULC
22 Adelaide St. West, 41st Floor
Toronto, Ontario M5H 4E3, Canada
www.Harlequin.com

Printed in U.S.A.

**Christy Jeffries** graduated from the University of California, Irvine, with a degree in criminology and received her Juris Doctor from California Western School of Law. But drafting court documents and working in law enforcement was merely an apprenticeship for her current career in the dynamic field of mommyhood and romance writing. Christy lives in Southern California with her patient husband, two sarcastic sons and a sweet husky who sheds appreciation all over her car and house.

### Books by Christy Jeffries

Visit the Author Profile page
at Harlequin.com for more titles.

To Tommy Thompson, everyone's favorite uncle. The first time I met you, you got a business call and told the person on the other end of the line that you couldn't talk right that second because you were about to do a shot of Cabo Wabo with your niece. Since that day, anytime you've introduced me to someone (and you seem to know *everyone*), the phrase *niece-in-law* has never been in your vocabulary. It's no wonder everyone in your family—especially your "grand-nephews"—adore you. You have the biggest heart and you make life more fun...

## Prologue

Nearly everyone in our small Montana town had attended some sort of event in the newly renovated Bronco Convention Center. But only one other couple had thrown an actual party inside of it. Of course, the last weekend in January wasn't exactly the time of year for a large outdoor gathering, and the crowd tonight was definitely a large one.

Everyone knows that when the beloved mayor invites the whole town to celebrate his thirtieth wedding anniversary, it's not a question of *if* you'll go. It's a question of what you should wear and who else is going to be sitting at your table. Sure, you could miss the annual Christmas tree lighting or a rodeo on occasion. Those types of events brought in enough tourists that your absence might go unnoticed. However, tonight's party celebrating Rafferty and Penny Smith was strictly for the locals. And anyone who was anyone in Bronco, Montana, had RSVP'd yes before the invitations were even printed.

"Thank you all for coming out to join me and Penny on this momentous occasion," Mayor Rafferty Smith began his speech welcoming everyone. The man was a great speaker and an even better storyteller. It was no wonder he kept getting reelected. "You know, when I first asked Penny to marry me, I wasn't sure she'd say yes. In fact, I don't think *she* even knew she was going to say yes. But we were just a couple of young kids in love back then, flying by the seats of our pants. We had no big plans other than making it through each day and having as much fun as we could. Nobody tells you how much work a marriage takes... I mean, nobody except all the boring adults who know better than you. But you ignore them because you've got too many stars in your eyes. Then, as time goes by and you begin to look back on all the ups and downs, all the good times and the bad, you begin to realize what you've actually accomplished. Personally, my biggest achievement is sharing the past thirty years with the woman I love."

Everyone oohed and aww'd as the mayor pulled his wife onto the stage beside him. "Penny, you've stuck by my side all this time and there is nothing I could give you that would even come close to everything you've given me these past years. But I couldn't show up here completely empty-handed." The crowd chuckled politely, then applauded as Rafferty presented his wife with a black velvet jewelry case. "They say pearls are traditional for the thirtieth anniversary, but if you ask me, there is nothing traditional about you, Penny Smith. Like this necklace, you are one of a kind and I can't wait to see what the next thirty years have in store for us."

Rafferty made a big show of fastening the stunning heirloom pearl necklace around Penny's neck, causing the guests to cheer uproariously when he hauled his wife into his arms for an over-the-top kiss.

Everyone in the crowd agreed—the party was already off to a fabulous start.

## Chapter One

Dylan Sanchez forced himself to come tonight because he didn't want to be the only business owner in Bronco who refused the mayor's invitation. Oh, and because his parents and siblings would've never let him hear the end of it if he'd skipped.

At the rate the Sanchez family was growing, though, it wasn't just the opinions of Dylan's two brothers and two sisters he had to contend with, either. He'd assumed that when his sisters got married and his brothers got engaged, they would find better things to do with their time than remind him that he was now the odd man out.

Clearly, he'd been wrong about that.

Not that Dylan wasn't proud to be the last Sanchez standing. Growing up in a competitive family, if he wasn't going to be the first one to do something, then he sure as hell was going to outlast everyone else. It was just that being surrounded by so many happy couples, talking about anniversaries and upcoming weddings, could start to wear on a happily single guy.

Plus, he hated crowded events.

"Aren't these tables only supposed to seat ten people?" Dylan muttered to his father. "How did we manage to get thirteen chairs crammed around one tiny space?"

"Thirteen chairs *and* a stroller," his brother Dante said as he rocked his and his fiancée Eloise's daughter back to sleep in her little buggy. Merry, Dylan's eight-week-old niece, was officially his favorite family member, and not just because she kept her opinions to herself.

A few minutes later, when Dylan mentioned the lack of elbow room, his sister Sofia replied, "Boone and I are going to sit with the rest of the Daltons once they pass out the cake. You can put up with being squished for that long, Dylan."

"Yeah, but I don't know how long I can put up with Felix stealing my beer." Dylan snatched the pint glass from his older brother's hand. "The bar's right over there if you want to go get your own."

Felix had the nerve to smile unapologetically. "Shari and I are going to head that way for another round as soon as she and Mom get done talking about bridal shower themes. In the meantime, you can share."

Uncle Stanley returned from the buffet line with two full plates and his fiancée, Winona Cobbs. As the older couple took their seats, there was even less space to move.

Dylan turned toward his sister Camilla. "I think your in-laws are looking for you."

"No they're not," Jordan Taylor, Camilla's husband, replied. "My dad and uncles are busy holding court with the mayor."

"If you need to get away from us, Dylan," Camilla said as she nodded discreetly at a table with several young women, "there's room over there."

"Stop trying to set me up. Between the car dealership and the new ranch, I don't have time for a girlfriend right now."

"When have you ever had time, Dyl?" Sofia asked. "Aren't you getting tired of the dating scene? You're not getting any younger."

"Uncle Stanley is eighty-seven and *he* just got engaged. So there's not exactly an age limit for someone getting married. In fact, I don't have to get married at all." Dylan knew he sounded defiant, possibly even stubborn. But the more his family talked about weddings, the more determined he became to stay single.

"Don't forget, kiddo, that I was already married once and there's nothing better than sharing your life with someone." Uncle Stanley, who'd been a widower for some time, turned to Winona. "Speaking of which, we should probably be setting our own wedding date soon."

Winona, a ninetysomething-year-old psychic who was prone to mystical statements, shrugged noncommittally. "We will when the time is right."

"You're not having second thoughts, are you?" Uncle Stanley asked, concern causing the wrinkles around his eyes to deepen.

Winona shook her head, her messy white bun tipping to one side. "Of course not. But love cannot be rushed. It *will* not be rushed." Then she pointed an age-spotted hand covered with several rings at Dylan. "But it cannot be avoided, either. Love always finds a way."

Dylan opened and closed his mouth several times, unsure of how to respond. Or if he should. He reclaimed his beer once again from his brother and drained the glass before changing the subject.

"Anyway, the ranch has me so busy lately, I hired two new salespeople for the dealership to cover for me. But January is normally a slow month for car sales. I need to think of something to get business moving again."

"You could try not spending so much time at Broken Down Ranch," one of his sisters suggested.

"It's called Broken *Road* Ranch," he corrected. His family had always been supportive of his dream to own land, but several of them had recently questioned his decision to own *this* particular property. The place was a bit of a fixer-upper and most of the buildings had seen better days. But it sat in one of the best spots in the valley and, hopefully, the grass would return this spring and make it look not so… well…run-down.

"What about a car wash?" Dante, the elementary

school teacher, suggested. "My school did one before summer break last year and made a decent amount."

Dylan frowned. "I don't need a onetime fundraiser. I need to get more people on my lot. But without being one of those cheesy salespeople who resort to gimmicks or corny commercials just to make a buck. You know how I hate public speaking."

"What about a game of hoops?" Their father had raised his children with a passion for sports. "We could do a tournament, like we do with the rec league. I'll be the referee."

Several people at their table groaned, including Dylan's mom, who had attended more than her share of basketball tournaments over the years.

"That would take an awful lot of time for people to form teams and have practices," their mom said. "You need to put something together sooner and you need a theme."

"Valentine's Day is coming up," Sofia said a bit too casually and all the women were very quick to agree. Suspicion caused the back of Dylan's neck to tingle.

"You guys want me to do something on a commercialized holiday created for the sole purpose of selling romance to people? What am I going to do? Have a Valentine's dance?" Dylan snorted at the absurdity. "No wait, maybe I should send everyone who wants to test-drive a car on a ride through a tunnel of love."

Uncle Stanley raised his hand. "I vote for the tunnel of love idea."

Dylan needed another drink. "Buying a vehicle is a big decision, you guys. When someone comes to my dealership, it's to make a practical purchase. They're not there for all that mushy stuff."

And neither was Dylan. He didn't do mushy. He certainly didn't do grand gestures like Mayor Smith had done up on the stage a few minutes ago when he'd given his wife that necklace in front of the whole town.

"Valentine's Day is one of the biggest nights of the year in the service industry," Camilla, who owned her own restaurant, pointed out. "Trust me, when it comes to gifts, some people want more than flowers and chocolates."

Dylan grimaced. "So I just get some big red bows and hoist up a new banner? Maybe dress up as Cupid and shoot arrows at the potential customers?"

Winona lifted her wineglass. "Lots of gals in this town wouldn't mind seeing the Sanchez brothers dressed up like Cupid and wearing nothing but a tiny white toga."

Thankfully, that suggestion got a resounding set of *noes* from Felix and Dante. Several more ideas were offered and rejected before Dylan excused himself to go to the bar while his family wore themselves out discussing the most absurd concepts that would never come to fruition. He told himself that he'd grab another beer, maybe a plate of food, and by the time he got back to the table, his family would have moved on to another subject.

However, Dylan got sidetracked talking with a few buddies about the upcoming baseball season, speaking to one of the city council members about a permit application for some electric vehicle charging

stations and checking the score on the college basketball game. When he returned to the party, he ran
into Mrs. Coss, the older lady who owned the antiques
mall next door to his dealership.

"I think it's a great idea, Dylan. I'll even be willing
to lend you a few pieces from my 1920s rolling pin collection as long as they're just used for display purposes."

He smiled politely despite his confusion. "What's
a great idea, Mrs. Coss?"

"The bake-off. Maybe I'll put out a shelf of my
older cookbooks and a rack of mid-century aprons to
do a little sidewalk sale." The band began playing their
rendition of the "Cha Cha Slide," and before Dylan
could ask her what she meant, Mrs. Coss said, "This
is my song. We'll talk more about cross-promotion
tomorrow." She patted him on the arm and dashed
onto the dance floor before he could say another word.

Dylan heard the word *bake-off* several more times
on his way back to the table. By the time he arrived
at his seat, most of his siblings and his mom were already gone, blending into the crowd. His dad was still
there, though, holding baby Merry and serenading
her with the off-key lyrics of the line dancing song.

"Where'd everyone go?" Dylan asked his dad.

"They're spreading the word about the bake-off."

Dylan's temples began pounding. "Please tell me
that this doesn't have anything to do with my dealership."

"Hey, Dylan," LuLu, the owner of his favorite BBQ
joint, called out from two tables over. "What's the
prize for the bake-off?"

His dad responded before Dylan could. "A year's worth of free mechanical service. Oil changes, new brakes, tire rotations, that sort of thing."

All the color drained from Dylan's face as he stared at his dad in shock. "I was gone for thirty minutes."

Apparently, thirty minutes was all it had taken for Dylan's entire family to come up with a harebrained idea to hold a Valentine's Day–themed bake-off at his place of business. Oh, *and* promise the winner a prize valued at potentially thousands of dollars. But it was too late to call the thing off. Gossip spread like wildfire in Bronco and Dylan was officially on the hook for a contest he hadn't authorized.

"Nobody even asked my permission," he told Dante, the first sibling who returned to the table.

"Have you met Mom and our sisters? You walked away midconversation. That's practically giving them your blessing to proceed however they see fit."

Dylan rolled his eyes. "It's a car dealership, not the set of some cooking show. You've seen my break room. I have an old microwave and a toaster that sets off the smoke alarm anytime I want a bagel. How do they think they're going to hold a bake-off there?"

"I don't know. Something about a giant party tent and one of Camilla's suppliers who rents out restaurant-grade ovens." Dante took his baby from their dad. "I wasn't really paying attention, man."

Could this evening get any worse? The pounding at Dylan's temples revved into a full headache and he was about to call it a night. But if he left the party now, what other crazy schemes would his family come up with in his absence? Needing to ward off the gossip and do damage control, he rose from the table.

Unfortunately, he didn't get more than two feet when the mayor thwarted his plans.

"Dylan!" Rafferty Smith reached out to enthusiastically shake Dylan's hand. "I hear we're holding an exciting town event at the dealership next month. Penny loves that British baking show, by the way. Obviously, I'd be honored to help judge the contest. I'll tell my assistant to clear my schedule for that day."

Okay, so having the mayor make an appearance at his dealership could actually be good for business. Plus, Dylan was in the middle of working on a bid proposal to supply the city officials with a fleet of vehicles. Since he didn't want to risk losing that contract, he had no choice but to clench his jaw, smile and act as though this ridiculous bake-off plan could actually work. That it wouldn't be nearly as embarrassing as him running around dressed like Cupid. "Great. It should be a lot of fun. I look forward to having you join us."

Mayor Smith then took a step closer and lowered his voice. "Just between us, any chance you happened to see a pearl necklace around here?"

"You mean like the one you gave your wife less than an hour ago?"

"Shh. Keep your voice down. Penny had it on when we were on the dance floor, but it must've fallen off somewhere. I'm trying to ask around discreetly because I don't want to cause a—"

"Attention, ladies and gentlemen," the lead singer of the band interrupted as he spoke into the microphone. "We have an announcement to make. If anyone finds a pearl necklace, please bring it up to the stage so we can reunite it with its owner."

The crowd's hushed murmurs quickly grew louder as everyone realized whose necklace had gone missing. Rafferty Smith muttered, "So much for doing anything discreetly in this town," before striding away.

Dylan couldn't agree more.

Surely someone would find Penny's necklace soon. Dylan doubted his own reputation as a serious businessman would be recovered as easily.

Robin Abernathy was better on the back of a horse than she was in front of an oven. But she'd been known to have a few tricks up her sleeve when it came to the kitchen. Or at least a few recipes.

Okay. Two recipes. One of which, fortunately, was a batch of cookies. Besides, she didn't want to actually win the Valentine's Day bake-off. She just wanted to get one of the judges to notice her.

She parked one of the ranch trucks at the curb in front of Bronco Motors, then stared at her reflection in the rearview mirror. Her summer tan had long faded, and her complexion could benefit from a swipe of blusher. Too bad she didn't own any makeup. She dug around in her purse and came up with a tube of colorless lip balm. Oh well. She yanked the elastic band out of her hair, ditching her usual ponytail. Maybe she'd look more feminine with her hair down.

For the first time in thirty-one years, Robin asked herself why she couldn't be better at the whole flirtation thing. Probably because she spent too much time with her brothers and the other cowboys out on her family's ranch. If she couldn't find the time to go out on many dates, then she certainly didn't have the time to put much effort into her appearance. If a guy didn't appreciate her for being herself, what was the point in bothering with a second date?

But that was before Dylan Sanchez had smiled at her during Bronco's annual Christmas tree lighting event. She hadn't been able to stop thinking of the man since then.

She'd planned to casually run into him at the Smiths' anniversary party, but a last-minute emergency with one of her client's horses had kept her away. Maybe it was better this way since his recently announced bake-off might prove to be a better opportunity to talk to the man without such a huge crush of people around.

As if on cue, she saw him striding across the dealership lot and heading into the office. Robin wasn't used to the feeling of butterflies in her stomach because it was rare that her nerves got the best of her. Before she could overthink what she was about to do, she exited the truck and slammed the driver's door, closing off any doubt and leaving it behind her.

*You can do this.* Gripping the printed flyer tighter in her fist, she entered the building that served as a couple of offices and a showroom for a brand-new 4x4 truck. She'd purposely picked a time when she thought the dealership wouldn't be busy and, from what she could see, it appeared she'd planned well. Nobody else was around.

Dylan's voice made its way through an open door and then a second voice responded from what sounded like a speakerphone. Not wanting to interrupt his call, she casually walked around the vehicle on display, reading the information on the back window sticker.

It wasn't that she was trying to eavesdrop, but it was hard not to hear him in his office ten feet away. It only took her a few moments to figure out the extent of the conversation. His small herd had been over-grazing in the same spot for years and he couldn't move them until he had time to repair some fences. The other voice clearly belonged to a fertilizer sales-man trying to convince Dylan to invest in an untested anti-erosion soil product. The last phrase sent a warn-ing bell to Robin's brain and she found herself inch-ing closer to the office.

Dylan was pacing back and forth in the small space, the lines on his forehead deeply grooved. When he caught sight of her, she immediately took a step back, but not before she saw his face transform from concern to a veneer of charm and grace.

"Let me call you back, Tony," he said as Robin pretended to be absorbed in reading about all the off-road features listed on the truck's sticker price.

"Welcome to Bronco Motors," Dylan told her with that same smile and those same cheek dimples that she'd been seeing in her dreams the past several weeks. "Are you interested in trying this out?"

She almost said yes, then realized he was talking

about the car between them. "Oh, um, not today. I came to sign up for the bake-off."

She held up the flyer, as if to prove that was her sole intention in coming here.

If Dylan was disappointed that she wasn't there to buy a car, he covered it well. "Right. So full disclosure, my mom and sisters did the flyers this past week and posted them all over social media before I even got a chance to create any sort of official sign-up or even come up with contest rules. I wasn't really prepared for the amount of interest I've already gotten." He walked over to an empty reception desk and retrieved a clipboard. "So I've just been having people put their contact information on this sheet. We'll reach out when we have all the details finalized."

Whoa. Up close, the man smelled even better than he looked. Trying not to let the scent of his cologne go to her head, Robin took the clipboard from him and it only took a quick glimpse at the other names on the list to see that it was all women. Apparently, she wasn't the only one in town who wanted an excuse to get up close and personal with the last single Sanchez brother.

She paused with the pen in her hand. This was so foolish. What was she even doing here? Someone like her wouldn't have a chance of winning a baking contest or attracting a guy like Dylan. But as he stood there watching, another thought occurred to her. He'd just asked her if she wanted to go for a test-drive. Her parents bought all their ranch vehicles from this dealership, including several of this exact same model. If Dylan knew who she was, then he would know that Robin wouldn't need to test-drive a car she often used at work.

Which meant he had no idea who she was.

Robin wasn't sure if she should be relieved or offended. Until he added, "I should probably warn you that the bake-off is on Valentine's Day. In case you're already busy that day. Or, you know, have plans."

She looked up quickly and was rewarded with the sexiest smile and the most smoldering pair of brown eyes she'd ever seen. At least this close. Was he suggesting that she might have some sort of date for the most romantic day of the year? Her sister, Stacy, teased her about being oblivious to men flirting with her. Was this one of those times?

Since Robin couldn't just stand there staring at him in confusion, she mumbled what she hoped sounded like, "No, I'm available." Or at least it would've sounded like that if her tongue wasn't all tied up in knots.

She scribbled her name on the list, along with her cell number and email address. Her face was flushed with heat by the time she returned the clipboard to him, but he didn't give it so much as a glance before tucking it under his arm.

His phone rang from his pocket and he pulled it out long enough to glance at the screen and then silence it.

"I should probably let you get back to work," she said, jumping on the excuse to get away before she did or said something else that made her seem like a lovesick fool.

"Only if you're sure I can't interest you in a test-drive."

No, Robin wasn't sure at all. But her whole goal in coming here today was to meet the man in person and see if this crush she'd developed on him from afar was just as foolhardy as she'd been telling herself. And the answer was yes.

"Nope, I'm all set," she said, pivoting to leave. Before she executed a full turn, though, she stopped in her tracks. "Actually. I know this is none of my business, but someone needs to stop you from making a huge mistake."

## Chapter Two

Dylan's head jerked in response to her words and his skin bristled. He was already sensitive to his family's teasing about not knowing the first thing when it came to ranching. He didn't need some stranger offering him unsolicited advice, as well.

"I have a feeling this mistake you're referring to has nothing to do with the bake-off." Although, Dylan was pretty sure that this silly contest was already proving to be more trouble than it was worth.

"No. It's about the untested fertilizer product that you really shouldn't be using."

"Thank you for your concern, but I assure you I have it well under control. Tony, the salesman I was talking to, has advanced degrees in chemistry and geology and knows quite a bit about soil erosion. I doubt he'd steer me wrong."

"Come on." The blonde woman put her hands on her hips, the bake-off flyer now crumpled in her fist. "It doesn't take a degree to know what works for a herd of cattle and what doesn't. But, hey, what do I know about ranching?"

She said it with such confidence, as though she was accustomed to people eagerly taking her advice. She also said it with enough sarcasm to suggest that he should know who she was. Dylan blinked several times as he tried to place her, but he was pretty sure he'd remember meeting someone with a face like that. A face that was almost more enhanced by the lack of makeup.

Hoping for a clue, he glanced at the clipboard. Robin *Abernathy*.

Hell. How had he missed that? She must be one of the younger sisters that graduated high school after he did.

The Abernathys were the second richest ranching family in Bronco, right after the Taylors, his brother-in-law's family. Dylan didn't like the trail of unease making its way through his body. Although he'd grown up in a ranching town and thought of himself as being familiar with horses and cattle all his life, his dad was a postal worker and his mom was a hairdresser. Besides the occasional sleepover with friends when he was in high school, Dylan never really spent any significant amount of time on a ranch. Until he found himself owning one.

Curiosity, though, outweighed his embarrassment and he couldn't stop himself from asking, "Why would it be a mistake?"

Robin sighed, as though she had to explain something to a child. "I've heard of his product and even though it's a hot new trend, what your salesman isn't telling you is that one of the main chemicals they add to the fertilizer has proven to be harmful to some breeds of cattle. Especially maternal cattle."

She said the last part as though she was already aware that the previous owner of the Broken Road Ranch had left Dylan with a herd primarily consisting of female cows. It was something Dylan was still kicking himself for overlooking.

"Plus, that brand of fertilizer is way overpriced. You'd be better off spending your money and time on repairing your fences or even using a feedlot until the land has time to be properly restored."

The problem was that he was getting low on time. He needed a quick fix.

"There's no quick fix," Robin said as though she was reading his mind. "Ranching is time-consuming."

"I'm aware of that," he said a bit too quickly. A bit too defensively. Deep down, he knew that she was only trying to offer some friendly advice. However, he was already sensitive to the fact that he was in way over his head. It didn't help that someone from the successful Abernathy family was the one pointing it out.

Admitting that he needed help was a tough pill to swallow. The only thing worse would be admitting defeat and losing the ranch completely. Dylan was going to have to suck it up and take whatever advice he could get at this point. But that didn't mean he had to like it.

He crossed his arms in front of his chest. "So then why would Tony give me the exact opposite advice?"

Robin bit her lower lip, as if considering her words. After a weighty pause, she finally said, "Not everyone in this world is truthful if their paycheck depends on making a commission."

"That's certainly a polite way of saying you can't trust a salesperson." He'd always enjoyed making deals, but sometimes the used car salesmen jokes hit a little too close to home. "Not all of us are liars looking to make a quick buck."

The way Robin scrunched her nose would've been adorable if her doubtful expression wasn't directed at him. "Nobody called *you* a liar or said *you* were untrustworthy. But tell me again why you're having a Valentine's Day bake-off at a car dealership. Is it because you have so much free time on your hands running two businesses that you decided to throw in hosting a community event just for a fun little challenge?"

If her words were intended as a blow to his ego, she definitely hit the mark. The building tension in his shoulders and neck, as well as her know-it-all smirk, made him more defensive. Or at least competitive enough to play along with her sarcastic comment. "Maybe it's because I simply enjoy having a pretty woman like you cook for me."

She gasped and her high cheekbones turned a rosy shade of pink.

Realizing how sexist his words sounded, he immediately held up his palms. "I didn't mean it like that!"

She shifted on her feet. Her formfitting jeans were tucked into tan cowboy boots, making her long legs seem even longer. "H-how did you mean it?"

"Not that I expect a pretty woman, or any woman, to cook for me. You can ask my mom and my sisters, I'm actually a pretty decent cook. In my family, we take turns making Sunday dinner and I can hold my own."

"I know. Eloise Taylor told me about your flaming fajita incident." Robin pointed at his eyebrows. "They grew back nicely, by the way."

He rubbed the bridge of his nose, which probably only drew more attention to his brows. "It was a little fire and it only happened that one time... Wait. You're friends with my brother's fiancée?"

His question was unnecessary, though. Of course the Abernathys knew the Taylors. The wealthy families of Bronco Heights all tended to run in the same circles. But he hadn't recognized Robin when she first walked in, and he was pretty sure he would've remembered if Eloise had a hot friend who was also an experienced rancher. Or at least Dylan's mom and sisters would've mentioned it. They were always trying to set him up with someone.

"I'm actually one of her clients. She's working on a marketing campaign for my company."

"You have a company?" Why was he repeating everything she said? "I mean, I assumed you worked for your family since you act like you know so much about ranching."

"I know a lot about ranching because I grew up working on my family's ranch. But I also own my own business. Rein Rejuvenation. It's a line of horse therapeutics I created…" Robin trailed off as a young woman walked into the dealership office. The newcomer's high heels clacked against the tile floors despite the fact that it definitely wasn't high heel weather outside.

"Hi, I'm here to enter the bake-off," the woman said excitedly.

"Of course. Here you go." Dylan handed her the clipboard he was still holding. When he turned back to Robin she was already walking toward the exit.

"Robin, hold up," he called across the small showroom floor as he took long strides to catch her. She paused, her head tilted as though she was confused about why he was running after her. Or maybe she was just insulted and eager to get away.

"Before you leave, I wanted to say thanks for your advice about the fertilizer and…everything. I think I'm going to reach out to some of my neighbors and see who they use for fence repairs."

If Dylan was being honest, the reason he hadn't reached out to them before now was the same reason he'd gotten all defensive with Robin earlier. He didn't want people thinking that he had no idea what he was doing. Plus, he wanted to do the work himself. Not hire someone to do it for him.

"I'm sure they'd be willing to make some suggestions. There's a lot to learn about the ins and outs of ranching, but you have to be open to asking for help."

Again, Robin seemed to be reading his mind. Or else issuing a challenge.

It was a challenge he knew better than to accept. In spite of that, Dylan fired back, "Are you offering to teach me?"

"If you're willing to learn," she replied cheekily.

Dylan found Robin attractive before, but her self-assurance now had him fully intrigued.

"Cool truck." The young woman he'd left with the clipboard made her way over to them. "I'd love to take it for a test-drive."

When his family had concocted this ridiculous bake-off scheme, they'd insisted on people signing up in person instead of online. He'd agreed thinking it would get more people stopping by the dealership, which ultimately was the goal. But at this exact second, Dylan wished one of the other salespeople was here to help.

"Don't let me keep you from your customer." The way Robin said the word *customer* sounded as though she wanted to use air quotes. But maybe that was just Dylan's imagination because her smile toward the woman looked genuine.

As Robin turned toward the door, he reminded himself that he was a professional at his place of business. Now wasn't the time to be admiring the view of her rear end in those jeans. Clearing his throat, he forced himself to give a polite wave and simply say, "I'll be in touch about the bake-off."

Dylan suddenly had the urge to taste anything Robin Abernathy put in front of him.

"So, he had no idea who you were?" Stacy Abernathy practically shouted the question inside Bronco Java and Juice, causing the other customers to turn in their direction.

Wincing, Robin immediately shushed her sister. "Once he saw my name, he knew who I was. But no, he didn't recognize me."

Despite the fact that Robin wanted to saddle her favorite horse and go for a long ride to forget about all the awkward moments at the dealership earlier today, she and her sister had a standing coffee date every Monday after school let out.

Stacy took a sip of her triple espresso—she always got a triple when her first graders had an especially rough day. "Didn't you two go to high school together?"

"No, I graduated the same year as Dante Sanchez. Dylan was a couple years ahead of me."

"So when he smiled at you during the tree lighting, he had no idea who you were?"

Robin shrugged. At the beginning of December, the entire town—along with plenty of tourists—attended the holiday celebration at the park in the center of Bronco Heights. "It was crowded and there was a lot going on that night. He's a charming guy with a reputation for being a huge flirt. I guess he smiles that way at everyone."

"But that was the night you fell for him."

"I didn't *fall* for him, Stacy. I just developed a tiny

little crush." Robin used her thumb and forefinger to indicate the smallest amount possible. "Very tiny. Barely even a crush. More like he merely caught my interest. From afar. We've never even had a conversation up until two hours ago."

"Now I feel stupid for talking you into approaching him at all."

"Don't blame yourself." Robin made a swatting gesture at the air. "When has anyone ever talked me into doing anything? I'm a big girl and I make my own decisions."

"Yeah, but I was the one who told you that Dante and Dylan Sanchez aren't as big of flirts as people make them out to be." Stacy and Dante were both teachers at Bronco Elementary and Robin had, in fact, slightly relied on her sister's assessment of the brothers.

In order for Robin to feel as though she were in control, though, she also needed to shoulder some of the responsibility. "But I was the one who convinced myself that Dylan noticed me that night and that he could possibly be interested."

"That's because I might have made the suggestion in the first place," Stacy argued. "However, in my defense, Dante seemed to be easily snatched off the market by Eloise when she unexpectedly returned to town a few months ago. It was fair to assume that Dylan wouldn't be so hard to get, either."

"Speaking of Dante, here comes Eloise," Robin said as soon as she caught sight of her friend pushing a stroller past the window outside. "Don't mention anything about this to her."

"Hey, ladies, thanks for letting me crash your coffee date," Eloise Taylor said a few moments later when she parked the stroller by their table. "I'm technically still on maternity leave, but I got the proofs back from the photo shoot of that magnetic horse blanket and I couldn't wait to show you, Robin. Also, don't ever fall in love with the fixer-upper your Realtor shows you and move in the second you close escrow. The construction crew remodeling our downstairs bathroom is currently jackhammering the tile. Merry can sleep right through the noise, but I can't hear myself think let alone do a conference call. I desperately needed a latte. So what's going on with you two?"

"Well, I'm currently questioning my poor decision to take my first graders on a field trip to the wildlife center during birthing season and Robin is trying to make me feel better by telling me about how she made a fool of herself in front of your future brother-in-law."

Robin shot Stacy a scathing look.

Eloise made a dismissive motion with her hand. "Felix is a veterinarian, Robin. I'm sure he knows the difference between dog flatulence and human flatulence."

"Not *that* brother-in-law," Stacy corrected with a chuckle. "But now I don't have to ask how Bandit did at his deworming treatment."

"Oh, were you guys talking about Dylan, then?" Eloise dropped into the empty chair, sitting on the edge. "What happened?"

Silently cursing Stacy for bringing it up, Robin resisted the urge to drop her forehead into the palm of her hand. "On a whim, I stopped by the dealership to sign up for the bake-off."

"Really?" Eloise asked. "I didn't know you baked."

"She doesn't," Stacy replied.

"Yes, I do," Robin corrected. "Sometimes. Once in a while. Stop looking at me like that, Stacy, and drink your coffee."

A teenage barista with purple dyed hair came over to the table and asked Eloise if she wanted her usual. When the girl left, Robin hoped to change the subject, but Eloise was too fast.

"Was it crowded at the dealership when you went?"

Okay, Robin could at least answer this question easily enough. "Not when I was there, but there were already quite a few names on the list. And another woman came in when I was leaving. Why? Is everyone expecting a big turnout?"

If there were too many contestants, Robin could bow out gracefully and still save face.

"Nobody knows what to expect yet. Although, there's been some speculation on how many legitimate bakers will sign up and how many young single women will go in just to offer Dylan their phone number and…" Eloise's eyes widened with realization. "Oh my gosh, Robin, is that why you entered the contest?"

"No!" Robin said at the exact same time Stacy said, "Yep!"

Eloise looked between the two sisters.

Robin wanted to sink lower in her chair, but she forced herself to sit up straighter. "Okay, fine. Maybe I just wanted to test the waters and see what would happen if we talked in person. But he didn't know who I was."

Eloise frowned. "How does he not know who you are? Everyone knows the Abernathys. Didn't your family just buy a bunch of work trucks for the ranch? I remember Dante going in one weekend back in November to help Dylan with all the paperwork."

"Except Robin doesn't leave the ranch as much as the rest of us," Stacy pointed out. "Or at least she hasn't these past couple of years when she's been too busy working on her products."

"It's not like I'm a hermit," Robin corrected her sister. "I go to the feedstore and to other ranches. And I travel for some conferences and rodeos. I just don't have a lot of extra time for the Bronco social scene."

"Bronco has a social scene?" The barista set Eloise's latte on the table. She was wearing a nose ring and an I <3 NY pin on her apron. Her name tag said Solar. "Could've fooled me. My college acceptance letters can't come soon enough."

The three women all smiled indulgently at the teen. "We all thought the same thing when we were your age," Eloise told her. "But somehow we all ended up back here after college."

Actually, Robin had never wanted to escape Bronco. This was her home. Even when she'd gone off to get her degree, she'd picked the closest university so she could drive home every weekend to spend time with her horses. Which probably explained her lack of a social life.

When Solar left, Stacy asked, "So I'm still waiting to hear what happened after Dylan didn't recognize you. Did you at least correct him?"

"Sort of. When I walked in, I overheard him on the phone getting some bad advice. So before I left, I mentioned that he might want to reconsider taking that advice."

Stacy rolled her eyes.

Robin scowled. "What's that for?"

"Because you're a know-it-all and sometimes your so-called advice can come off a little condescending."

"There's nothing condescending about telling a man who has never owned a ranch that a fertilizer pumped up with all sorts of lab chemicals is going to have a negative effect on his breeders. I was saving him from an expensive and, frankly, potentially deadly mistake."

"If that's the tone you used," Stacy said as she nodded her head, "then I'd say it definitely came across as condescending. Possibly even bossy. Even if you were right."

"Of course I'm right."

Her sister pointed a finger. "See?"

Eloise drank some coffee and then sighed dramatically. "Man, I missed caffeine when I was pregnant. I feel like I'm making up for lost time. Anyway, regardless of how you presented the advice, I hope he took it."

"I hope so, too," Robin said, then tried to soften her tone so that it didn't sound quite so righteous. "Do you think he won't?"

"I'm still new to the Sanchez family and not really in a position to divulge their personal business. So I'm going to try to phrase this as delicately as I can because I only want what's best for my soon-to-be brother-in-law." Eloise looked up to the ceiling for several seconds as though she was trying to carefully choose her words. Then she blurted out, "Dylan has no idea what he's doing on that ranch and can use all the help he can get. But he's too damn stubborn and insists on doing everything himself. It's driving my cousin Jordan nuts and he's threatened to bring over the foreman and some ranch hands from the Triple T to help fix things. But Dylan won't hear of it. Dante says he's refusing everyone's advice, but maybe he'll listen to you."

Robin understood a person's need for independence. But she wasn't sure how she could make a difference when he wouldn't even listen to Jordan Taylor, who like her, was born into a cattle dynasty.

Stacy's drink was already halfway gone. "So did Dylan at least seem receptive to you?"

"Maybe?" Robin shrugged. "I guess we'll see."

She didn't want to tell them that he'd referred to her as "a pretty woman" or that she'd blushed like a fool when he'd said it. Nor did she want to tell them that she'd offered to teach him a few things if he was willing to learn. She'd already made the mistake of going to see the guy based solely on a smile he gave her in the park two months ago. She wasn't going to make the mistake of thinking he was flirting with her when he probably said the same thing to everyone who'd signed their names on his little clipboard.

All Robin knew was that she definitely wasn't going to follow through on the bake-off. She wasn't about to be lumped in with all the other women angling for his attention. In fact, she had every intention of trying to forget the entire incident.

Until her phone rang later that night.

She didn't have the number in her contacts and almost let it go to voice mail before realizing it might be someone at the rodeo arena calling about a horse. Despite the late hour and the fact that she was already in her pajamas, she answered professionally. "This is Robin."

"Hi, Robin, it's Dylan Sanchez." His voice sounded just as smooth and silky over the phone as it had in person. When it took her more than a few seconds to form a response, he added, "From Bronco Motors?"

As though she didn't know exactly who he was.

Robin grabbed her TV remote to mute the reality dating show she was watching. "Of course. Hi, how are you?"

"Busy. And I'm about to become a lot busier."

When he didn't elaborate, she made an assumption. "Too many bake-off contestants wanting to go for a test-drive today?"

"What? Oh. No. I mean, yes, there was a lot more traffic at the dealership than we usually get on a Monday in February. But I was actually referring to my ranch."

Wait. So he *wasn't* calling to update her on the bake-off rules?

As if he knew what she was thinking, he said, "I

hope you don't mind that I got your number off the sign-up sheet. But I was hoping I could pick your brain about the best types of feedlots."

"Um…" She stared at the frozen image on her TV, wishing she hadn't paused the show at the exact moment when the couple was sharing their first kiss. She scrambled to push the off button and clear the visual from her mind. "Go for it."

"So I was trying to research how much they cost. But then I read about this option involving fostering a herd with a neighboring ranch. I haven't started asking around yet, but I'll probably need to move the cattle myself and, uh, I've never really done that before. How many hands do you think I'll need to hire?"

"How many cattle are we talking about?"

"Thirty-five."

"You can probably get away with only using two riders."

"Right." He chuckled and she could almost imagine him on the other end of the line, running a hand through his thick, short-cropped dark hair. Was he standing in his office this late at night? Or was he home, in bed like she was? "But what if one of us isn't all that experienced?"

Robin gulped, then shook her head to clear the intimate image.

"At riding?" she asked. Because there was no way Dylan Sanchez wasn't experienced at things in the bedroom.

"At riding…" He paused a few more beats then finally said, "And at asking for help when I need it."

Whoa. So this was really happening. As much as Robin wished his motive for reaching out was to ask her out on a date, she knew better than to expect immediate results. Like training a horse, the first step was to get him to trust her. Not that she should be making that comparison.

Still.

The supposedly stubborn Dylan Sanchez was actually calling *her* for advice. Before she could consider her sister's earlier comments about sounding too arrogant, Robin said, "You've definitely come to the right person."

## Chapter Three

Dylan thought about the best way to respond to Robin's confident statement. His first impression of her today was that she was gorgeous. His second impression was that she was gorgeous *and* she was a know-it-all.

By the time she'd left his dealership, though, he was convinced that women who were gorgeous know-it-alls likely had egos to match. But he'd spent the afternoon researching her advice and came to the conclusion that maybe it wouldn't hurt him to at least listen to her.

"Well, you did offer to teach me a thing or two," he finally replied to Robin.

"I did. But it also depends on what kind of help you're looking for." Robin's voice was raspy, but feminine, and Dylan liked the sound of it a bit more than he should. He'd noticed it earlier today when she'd introduced herself. Over the phone, though, it had an even stronger pull. Probably because he couldn't see her in person, forcing him to use his imagination to envision her full pink lips pronouncing each word. "If you're looking for a ranch hand, then you should know that I don't work for free. But if you're hoping for some neighborly advice, then I don't mind giving you my experienced opinion."

"I would never dream of asking you for free help. I'd obviously buy you lunch." Either Dylan's joke fell flat, or Robin Abernathy was really going to make him earn it. When she didn't reply, he added, "To be honest, what I really need is for someone who knows a lot more about ranching than I do to come out and make an overall assessment for me. I started a to-do list, but every time I turn around, I have to add another chore to it. Now I'm at the point where I don't even know which task I should tackle first. I guess, more than anything, I need someone to steer me in the right direction."

"If there's one thing I know how to do, it's steer something, or in your case *someone*, in the right direction. At least according to my brothers. But I have to ask, Dylan…" Robin paused as though she was trying to figure out how to phrase her question. "Why haven't you talked to Jordan Taylor or Boone Dalton about helping you with any of this?"

Jordan's family owned Taylor Beef and their ranch, the Triple T, was the biggest cattle operation in Montana. Boone worked with his family on Dalton's Grange, which was also an impressive ranch, even if some of Bronco's elite still considered the Daltons to be "new money."

Dylan exhaled, hoping it didn't sound like a sigh. "Trust me, they've talked to me about it plenty. My brothers-in-law, as well as everyone else in my family, have felt free to give me their opinions. At length. And while Jordan and Boone might have questionable skills on the basketball court, I'd never doubt their ranching abilities. However…my family hasn't exactly been optimistic of my recent endeavor."

"Really? Because Eloise gave me the impression that the entire Sanchez family is ultra supportive."

"Supportive, yes. In fact, sometimes they're a little *too* supportive." Dylan was now holding a bake-off contest, thanks to them. "But that's different than being optimistic. Long story short, nobody in my family thought acquiring Broken Road Ranch was a good idea. Obviously, they don't want me to fail at it and know how I get when I make up my mind to do something. But if they can throw in a few *I-told-you-so*'s along the way, they're going to. I guess you can say that I don't want to give them the opportunity."

"How did you acquire the ranch anyway? I heard a rumor about some sort of trade you made with the previous owner."

If Dylan could keep Robin's curiosity piqued, then he might have a shot. "I'll tell you what. Why don't you come by the ranch tomorrow and I'll fill you in on the entire history, as well as anything else you may want to know."

"Fine." Robin's tone was hard to gauge until she added, "But remember that I was promised a free lunch if I help."

Dylan ended up buying her breakfast.

"Thanks for stopping by so early," he told Robin the following morning when she got out of a newer model truck with the Bonnie B logo on the side. Yep, he'd definitely sold this same vehicle to her family just last November. All the more reason why he felt foolish for not recognizing her yesterday. "I have to leave by nine to get back to the dealership, but I picked up some muffins from Bean & Biscotti."

"I'm not going to say no to anything from Bean & Biscotti," Robin said as she scanned the barn and the broken fencing he hadn't had time to fix yet. "But just based on my first impressions driving up, I might need to raise my consulting fees."

Great. Dylan normally avoided asking for input because he was getting pretty tired of people telling him exactly what he didn't want to hear. He couldn't stop himself from sounding like a petulant child when he said, "It's really not that bad."

"I didn't say it was bad." Robin shoved her hands in the back pockets of her jeans, which caused her small, but round breasts to push out of her sheepskin coat. "It's just going to require a lot of time and energy."

"I've got the energy, but I'm a little short on time at the moment. Or at least, I am until I hire an office manager for the dealership." He glanced at his watch. "That's why I need to be back by nine. I have someone coming in for an interview. So do you want the full tour?"

"No need. I pulled up some land reports online and already made a couple of phone calls to your neighbors."

Dylan took a step back. "You did what?"

If he had wanted someone else coming in to usurp him and calling all the shots, he could've just asked one of his brothers-in-law to do it.

"I called the people who own the neighboring ranches." She pointed to the white bakery box balanced on a log fence post. "Are those the muffins?"

"No, I understood what you said. I guess I'm trying to understand *why* you did that."

"To get a better understanding of what we're dealing with. Are you telling me that you never called them when you bought the property?" Robin walked toward the fence post and Dylan found himself following.

"I mean, I didn't make a formal call because I've met them before around town at council meetings and business events. I even danced with Mildred Epson at the mayor's anniversary party."

"Yes, she told me. She said you asked about the hatchback you sold her great-grandson before he went off to college and informed me that you can two-step like nobody's business. But she also said you never brought up the disputed acres adjacent to Hardy's Creek."

"What dispute? It's on my property. At least according to the parcel maps."

"So that's your first lesson from me," Robin said as she helped herself to the box of baked goods. "Learn about the land's history and the people who owned it before you."

"How's this supposed to be a lesson? I'm still completely confused." He tilted his head as he watched her angle the top of the muffin into her mouth and take a bite right out of the center. "And who eats a muffin like that?"

"Did you ask Hank Hardy anything about the property before you bought it?" Robin asked, looking down at the baked good in her hand. "Also, the center is the best part. Why wouldn't I eat it?"

"You're supposed to peel back the paper first, like this." He took the muffin out of her hand and gently unwrapped it so the entire thing was exposed. When he passed it back to her, his fingers slightly brushed hers, sending a current of electricity through him. He cleared his throat. "Besides, I didn't exactly buy the ranch. It was signed over to me."

"Why would Hank Hardy just give you a ranch?"

"He didn't give it to me outright. But, according to him, he wasn't getting any younger and didn't think he'd be able to stand another snowy winter. His plan was to retire and drive across the country with a travel trailer, but he wanted to do it in a new truck. We made a bargain. He deeded the property to me, and I gave him the title to one of my trucks."

She finished off the muffin before asking, "Did you ever get an appraisal done?"

"Sort of. One of my buddies from college is a property agent with the state and ran some comps."

"So then you know that two hundred acres with outbuildings and a herd of thirty-five cows is still worth significantly more than that top-of-the-line 4x4 on your showroom floor. Even with all the bells and whistles."

"Thank you," Dylan exclaimed. "Could you please explain to everyone else in town that I got a smoking deal for my beef ranch?"

"No." She shook her head, her blond ponytail bouncing in the breeze.

"Why not?"

"Because you got a horrible deal for a beef ranch. Why do you think the herd that came with it was primarily female?"

"I figured ol' Hank was too kind to slaughter them."

"Maybe. But he also wasn't legally allowed to. The land is designated as a conservation easement."

"I'm not a total idiot, Robin. My friend informed me of that. I can only use the land for agricultural purposes. With the exception of rebuilding the main house and the outbuildings, I can never turn the property into something else or sell it to developers."

"In a normal conservation easement, that'd be correct. But this particular property is actually part of an agreement with several other ranches in the area limiting how the land can be used. Think of it as a no-competition clause put in place by all the neighbors. Or at least their ancestors. It's rare, but it happens. It used to happen a lot more a hundred years ago when ranchers were fighting over the grazing rights of their cattle and sheep herds."

"Sheep?" Dylan felt the blood drain from his face. Sure, the fluffy animals were cute and he loved the wool one of them had likely provided for the jacket he was currently wearing. But that didn't mean he wanted to raise them himself.

Robin must've been able to read the panic on his face because she giggled, which was exactly how his siblings would've responded if they were here.

"Don't worry." Robin had to pause to smother another bubble of laughter. "It doesn't have to be sheep. You can have any type of livestock you want on the land. There's just a slight catch. Your easement restriction is that any livestock over the age of nine months can't be sold for food. That means no beef or dairy cattle."

All of the air seemed to whoosh out of Dylan's lungs, taking his big plans and dreams right along with it. "But those are the kinds of cattle that make money."

"You're really going to make me earn this free breakfast, aren't you?" The smile Robin had been trying to hold back was now a full-fledged smirk. She reached for another muffin then said, "*Nine months* is the key term. You can still have an active breeding program, which can also be quite lucrative given the cows I see out on that pasture are maternal breeds. That means they're moderately sized and genetically predisposed to birthing calves. There are plenty of smaller ranches around here that don't have the resources to both breed *and* raise young calves. There's a steady market for herd replacements once a calf is weaned. You can also supply cattle to be used at nearby rodeos and charge rental fees. When I spoke with Mrs. Epson, she said that's what Hank's family used to do before he inherited the land. They made a pretty good living at it, too."

"Hank never disclosed any of that to me."

"Would you have taken the deal if he had?"

"Probably." Dylan cupped his hands against his forehead to block out the sun now blasting through the twin peaks of the snowcapped mountains in the distance. "I mean, it's pretty hard to top that view."

Robin paused with the center of the muffin halfway to her mouth and Dylan felt the weight of her stare. It reminded him of the weight of a different woman's judgment from the past that he still carried with him today. He dropped his arms to his sides and shrugged.

"I suppose *you* might be able to top it. Obviously, the Broken Road Ranch would never compare to something as vast and valuable as the Bonnie B. Yet, for a middle-class boy raised in a tract home in the Valley, there are times I have to pinch myself at the realization that this is all mine." Dylan pointed beyond the pastures toward a rising grove of trees. "See the creek that winds down from the mountain? When spring comes and the snowpacks start melting, it'll flow like a river all the way down here, passing only a few hundred yards behind the barn. Even on my most profitable days at the dealership, I've never felt as fulfilled as I do when I'm standing in this exact spot.

Nobody dreams of becoming a car salesman, Robin. At least, I didn't. Luckily, I've been good at it. Growing up in Bronco, though, you know as well as I do that success is often judged by the size of one's ranch. One of my biggest goals in life—other than playing in the NBA—has been to own my own spread. The dealership has always been the means to that end. The truth is that I probably would've traded all the cars on my lot if Hank had asked me to. I can't seem to explain it, and trust me, I've tried. All I know is that this land is already a part of me. And that's why I'm damn well going to learn to run this place myself."

Robin's half-eaten muffin sat forgotten in her palm as she studied Dylan. Initially, his smile had charmed her and drawn her interest. His request for advice had only made her more curious. But the man's passion for his ranch had just rendered her downright speechless.

Something her siblings and favorite ranch hands claimed didn't happen very often.

"I think you just explained it perfectly," Robin said when she finally found her voice. She blinked several times to focus her thoughts. "Now that I know why you love the land, tell me what you want to see happen with it."

"Ultimately, I'd like to see it turn enough of a profit that I can justify spending more time out here than I do at Bronco Motors. In the meantime, I wouldn't mind getting the house fixed up a little more so I could start sleeping out here regularly."

Robin tilted her head. "I thought when Eloise and Dante were dating, you used to spend the night here all the time."

"Only a few nights, and I was miserable. But I'm sure Dante would've done the same thing for me."

"What do you mean?"

"I mean bringing a woman home is a lot less romantic when you share an apartment with your brother. So I took one for the team and pretended like I needed to be out here more than I did. Thank God those two finally stopped caring about the gossip and eventually settled in at the Heights Hotel before buying their house."

If Dylan's love for the land hadn't convinced her that he was a good guy, then the fact that he'd been willing to sacrifice his comfort for his brother and Eloise's relationship would've proved it. She glanced at the main house that looked as if the roof might collapse at any minute and knew that she wouldn't have slept a single night inside it.

But she was also stuck on Dylan's statement that Dante would've done the same for him. Not *had* done the same. *Would* have. Was Dylan implying he'd never brought a woman back to his apartment? With his reputation, the idea was hard to believe.

Not wanting to be too obvious, Robin asked, "Has it been an adjustment, living on your own now that your brother's moved out?"

"Only to my wallet. I haven't won as many bets now that we aren't watching any games together in the evenings. That reminds me, I need to look into getting cable service out here. Or at least a solid internet provider. My apartment lease is up in six weeks and I'll be living out here full time. I need to be able to live stream March Madness."

He pulled his cell phone out of his pocket and began tapping on the screen.

"What are you doing?" Robin asked.

He didn't look up as he kept typing. "Adding to my growing list of things that need to get done."

"Don't you think taking care of that roof might be a little more important than some college basketball tournament?" she asked.

Dylan squinted at her. "Can't they be equally important?"

Robin sighed. Either she was going to fully commit to helping him or she wasn't. He was a successful business owner in town and his family was well respected and well-liked. Dylan Sanchez also struck her as a very determined individual. There was no way he couldn't learn enough about ranching to at least get some things fixed up around here.

But twenty minutes into their tour of the outbuildings, Robin was rethinking that assessment.

He jerked his thumb toward several rows of metal bars and frowned. "I'm not sure who designed that corral or whatever it is, but it's too long and takes up way too much space on this end of the barn."

"That's a breeding chute," Robin explained. "The heifer is pinned up in this area with her head facing away. Then the bull comes in from that gate over there and…well…you can use your imagination."

Dylan shuddered. "I don't want to use my imagination."

Robin laughed at his obvious discomfort. "If you're going to have a working ranch, Dylan, you have to know how the mating mechanics work."

"I know how it works. Sort of. I just don't need the image seared in my brain. Can't the bull take the heifer out to nice pasture somewhere and maybe they eat some grass together and moo at each other before…you know…he shows her a good time?"

"He could. But that way might take a little longer. You're not squeamish about such matters, are you?"

"No. At least I don't think I will be. My brother Felix is a veterinarian so it's not like I've never seen a litter of puppies being born."

"Okay, the second thing you're going to learn from me is that birthing a calf is a bit more complicated."

Dylan's face was full of doubt. "Tell that to the mom dog who just delivered six puppies."

Robin didn't know whether to laugh at his naivete or to throw her hands up in the air and give up on this plan entirely.

Except she'd never been a quitter.

"You said you have to be at your office by nine. What's the rest of your day looking like?"

"It looks like I'm chasing my own tail." Dylan glanced at his watch. "After that interview and a conference call with the distribution plant, I have to be back here at noon to meet with a plumber. If you think this barn is in need of a complete overhaul, wait until you find out about the plumbing in the main house.

Later on, Camilla wants me to stop by her restaurant to check out some plans she and Sofia came up with for that bake-off thing they're making me do. I'll stop by the dealership again to work on a sales forecast report and check in with the salespeople and the service tech. Then I'll try to be back out here before dark for the evening feeding."

The bake-off they're *making* him do? Robin tucked that nugget of information away to think about later. "Would you mind if I stayed here and showed myself around the rest of the property? Maybe take some notes and figure out a game plan?"

"Are you kidding? I would love that. I found an old golf cart in the barn. And when I say old, I mean it's ancient. But Hank put some off-road tires on it and the battery can hold a charge for at least an hour." Dylan's phone pinged and he took it out of his pocket to look at the screen. "Sorry to run like this, but I really need to take off. Maybe you can call me later tonight and let me know what ends up on your to-do list."

Her heart did a little fluttering dance at the thought of another late-night conversation with him. But then reality settled in as her eyes landed on one of the broken grain silos inside the barn. "I'll probably still be working on it when you get back."

"It's going to be that long, huh?" His charming smile had finally returned, but it didn't quite meet his eyes. She could see that he was still overwhelmed but trying to play it off.

"No." She returned his grin, trying to offer him a little reassurance. "But it is going to be that detailed."

He lifted only one brow. "Detailed sounds expensive."

"It doesn't have to be if you know where and how to get a good deal."

The gleam of excitement finally returned to his eyes as his shoulders visibly relaxed. "You sound like a woman after my own heart."

His words hit a little too close to home and heat rose along her neck. Before it could spread to her cheeks, Robin said, "Let me just grab a notebook and my coffee out of my truck and I'll get started."

She took long, fast strides to get outside, the cool winter air a welcome to her overheightened senses. At least it was until she realized he was right behind her. His voice was like warm honey when he said, "Hey, Robin?"

Hearing her name on his lips caused her to stop in her tracks. But she didn't turn around. "Yeah?"

"Do you think we should talk about my overall budget before you get too invested in this?"

Her family was a little old-fashioned when it came to talking about money, which meant that they didn't. But he'd already brought the subject up vaguely when he'd mentioned his upbringing and how he relied on bets with his brother to make extra cash. She would definitely need to be sensitive to his financial concerns.

Clearing her throat, she said, "Of course."

He named a sum that was surprisingly higher than what she'd anticipated. Her eyes widened for a brief second before her mind started calculating all the best ways to reinvest it into the ranch.

However, Dylan must've read her expression differently because he jerked his chin a little higher. "What? You didn't think a boy from the Valley could have that much saved up?"

"No." She reached up to straighten her ponytail, as though she could regain her composure. "But I do think with that kind of money to throw around, you can definitely afford to buy me lunch."

## Chapter Four

Dylan felt like a champion when he somehow managed to eke out enough time to return to the ranch with takeout from Bronco Burgers. But he hesitated when he saw the plumber's truck parked next to Robin's. She was standing on the weathered front porch with the plumber, her mouth moving nonstop as the poor man furiously scribbled notes onto his clipboard.

Dylan looked upward in silent prayer. *Please save me from determined women who like to plan things on my behalf.* Grabbing the sack of food and a flimsy cardboard carrier holding cups of sweet tea, he tried not to think of how much this was going to cost him. Not in terms of money so much—although he didn't want to blow through his entire budget just yet—but in terms of pride. He was still annoyed with himself for not realizing that the property he'd acquired had a restricted covenant.

"Hey, Brad," Dylan said as he cautiously avoided the missing board on the second porch step. The middle-aged plumber was the power forward on Dylan's recreational basketball team and had done some remodel work on the restrooms at Bronco Motors last year. He also had a daughter graduating from high school in a few months and was hoping to get a good deal on a used car for her.

"There better be some extra French fries in there." Brad's pen paused long enough to point at the bag in Dylan's hand. Then he explained to Robin, "My wife is on a health kick, which means we're all on a health kick since all carbs are currently forbidden from entering our house."

"I've got extra fries, onion rings and a patty melt with your name on it. But you better not tell Monique that I'm the reason you didn't finish that kale salad she keeps packing you for lunch." Dylan set the food on the porch railing and noticed Robin's eyes eagerly follow the bag. She was tall and lean, but after seeing her dig into the bakery box this morning, it was clear she enjoyed eating. He had a feeling his gamble was about to pay off. "I probably should've called to ask your order, but I was in such a rush to get back here, I made an executive decision and got you the double bacon cheeseburger."

Robin lifted one perfectly arched brow. "With extra bacon?"

Dylan resisted the urge to pump his fist in the air,

his confidence restored. He might not be the most knowledgeable about cattle, but he still knew how to read people.

"I figured anyone who eats the top of the muffin first isn't going to want to scrimp on the bacon," Dylan said before turning to Brad. "You want to finish doing your walk-through or do you want to eat first?"

Brad cleared his throat. "Actually, Robin already showed me around and gave me an idea of what you guys were thinking."

*You guys?* That was a bit presumptuous considering that Dylan and Robin hadn't even talked about the plumbing yet. Not to mention that it was Dylan's property and ultimately his decision, not hers.

"Is that right?" Dylan put his hands on his hips. "Remind me of what *we* were thinking, Robin."

"One of the first things *we* noticed was the newer, county-issued water meter outside the barn. Which means Dylan is already tied into their sewer system." She opened the bag and began passing out the burgers before adding, "Technically."

"Yeah, technically." Dylan nodded in agreement despite the fact that he most definitely had not noticed the water meter outside the barn. But he appreciated her including him in the discovery. Or at least covering for him by making him sound less clueless than he clearly was.

Robin continued, "But the house still uses that old septic tank over there, which probably explains the weird smell coming from the kitchen faucet. So Dylan can either replace the forty-year-old septic system or he can convert to sewer, which might be cheaper at this point and require less maintenance."

Damn. There was another thing he'd completely missed. Granted, he'd grown up in town and had never dealt with a septic system. Dylan's frustration quickly gave way to relief, though, at the realization that he might not have to totally replumb the house to fix that funky stench. That might be a big time-saver.

He took the fries Robin handed to him and asked, "Any chance you talked to Brad about the irrigation system for the pastures, too?"

"As a matter of fact, I did." A corner of her mouth tilted into a smirk and she actually winked at him. Dylan didn't know whether to be aroused or annoyed at her boldness. But there was no doubt in his mind that Robin knew full well that he was reliant on her expert opinion.

"Robin thinks the system is tied into several wells that are fed by Hardy's Creek," Brad said before biting into his sandwich.

*Of course she does.* Dylan silently asked himself why he bothered having the plumber come out since Robin was apparently the expert on everything.

"You'll eventually want to have those checked out, Dylan." Robin reached for one of the cups of sweet tea. "But with how much rain we usually get in March, you won't need to worry about that until the end of spring. We'll put that further down on your to-do list." She hesitated a moment and assessed him. "Why aren't you eating?"

Dylan glanced at the uneaten food in his hands.

Normally, he would've made quick work of the burger, especially since he thought better when his belly was full. But something made him pause. "Because I'm still trying to figure something out. If all I need to do is convert the house to the already existing sewer system, then why was Brad taking so many notes when I pulled up?"

His friend had just shoved an entire onion ring into his mouth and had to finish chewing before he could respond. "We were working on an estimate?"

Again with the *we*. Wait. Why had Brad phrased it as a question?

"An estimate for what?"

"The roof. And some of the electrical wiring that's pretty shoddy."

"But you're a plumber," Dylan reminded him.

"Technically." There was that word again, making Dylan see dollar signs. Brad continued, "But I was just telling Robin about how I recently got my general contractor's license and I'm thinking of expanding my business to work with a few subcontractors."

Sure, Dylan had been rather cocky when he'd told Robin earlier this morning that he had the budget for making the improvements. But just because he had the money didn't mean he wanted to waste it. Even if he had no need to worry about the financial side of things, there was still an emotional investment he'd been looking forward to creating.

"I was actually planning to do some of that work myself," Dylan said as though it should have been obvious. "I mean, isn't that part of owning land? To build it with your own two hands?"

"If you were a homesteader from the eighteen hundreds and had limited resources and an abundance of time, then sure." Robin once again seemed to be studying him, sizing him up. "But nobody goes it alone anymore, Dylan. Doing everything by yourself would be too time-consuming and it's not always economically feasible."

He knew her words were practical, but he still had to swallow a lump of disappointment that his dream might not happen the way he'd hoped. There'd been a tug-of-war raging inside him these past few months and it felt as though reality was about to win.

Robin put her palm on his shoulder and something about her touch sent a wave of peace through him. "Just because your two hands aren't doing the actual work doesn't mean you won't be putting in plenty of blood, sweat and tears. If Brad is taking care of the house, that gives you more freedom to focus on everything else that needs your attention. Both on the ranch and at your dealership."

"Yeah, I heard about that bake-off you're holding." Brad's reminder of the upcoming competition made Dylan wince. "Monique wants to enter, but she's yet to master a carb-free recipe that wouldn't earn her last place. Like this lunch, though, that's another thing we're going to keep between us."

Robin used her fingers to make a zipper motion across her lips.

Since Dylan would rather talk about sky-high construction estimates than that ridiculous contest his family was organizing, he brought the conversation back to the chaos he could at least control. "Knock 20 percent off your labor costs and I won't say a word to Monique about anything you eat on the jobsite. Now walk me through what you guys have in mind."

When the plumber drove off, Robin was still slightly in shock. She'd never really dealt with the repair side of things on her family's ranch, but she'd watched enough home renovation shows to know how much a full kitchen remodel would cost.

Granted, Brad was slowly expanding his business and it would benefit the man to lower his prices in an effort to build his clientele. But clearly, Dylan Sanchez's smooth-talking skills were not limited to just women.

"Do you always get what you want, Dylan?" she asked as he browsed the plumbing fixtures catalog Brad had left him.

He lifted his head, a crease between his brows. "What do you mean?"

"I mean that you somehow managed to get Brad to agree to an amount that's nearly a third lower than the going rate. Plus, he's adding a complete teardown and rebuild of both the front and back porches to the roofing contract."

"No. What I *wanted* was to do the repairs myself. Hiring Brad to do it was actually a compromise."

Robin chuckled as she shook her head. "There's certainly nothing wrong with your work ethic, I'll give you that. But they were right about your stubbornness."

His brown eyes widened. "Who said I was stubborn?"

She bit her lower lip, wishing she could take back her words. Eloise had simply given her some insight into the Sanchez family, but Robin worried that if she admitted as much, it'd seem like they'd been gossiping. Or that she'd been fishing for information about him. Which she sort of had been doing.

"I've heard it mentioned around town," she said quickly, then changed the subject. "So how did the interview go?"

Dylan's smile was immediate and caused his whole face to relax. "Better than I could've hoped. I hired her right on the spot. She's starting tomorrow."

Her? Robin remembered the pretty young woman from yesterday and wasn't accustomed to the split second of jealousy that flashed through her. "She must be quite impressive."

"She is. I don't know if you've ever met Mac, Jordan Taylor's assistant. It's her older sister. They look so much alike, right down to the steel gray curls and penchant for bright colored sneakers. Mickie is just as feisty as her sister and twice as organized."

Robin let out the breath she didn't realize she'd been holding. She had no claim to Dylan, and it was silly of her to even allow a single possessive thought to cross her mind.

"I know you have to get back for a meeting," she told him. "But I made some other notes before Brad got here. Maybe we can touch base tomorrow and go over those?"

"Just bring your list tomorrow afternoon when we go to that wholesale home improvement store Brad recommended."

Robin looked behind her to see if he was speaking to someone else. Nope. She was the only one there. "When did we decide I was going with you?"

"When you told Brad that *we* needed to demo all that ugly brown tile in the shower before replacing the drain pan. You didn't think I was going to go pick out all the bathroom materials by myself, did you?"

Alarm bells went off inside her head. "But I don't know anything about color schemes and decorating and making things look pretty."

His eyes dropped to her feet and then took their time traveling up her body to her face. "You seem to be well-equipped to me."

An unfamiliar tingle raced along the back of her spine. But that only caused her earlier panic to spread, which made her stiffen in defiance. "Why? Because I'm a woman?"

"No, because you're hot as hell, yet you make it seem effortless."

Her defensiveness vanished and she was only left with the tingling sensation as she tried to explain. "It's effortless because I literally put zero effort into being this...oh."

"You're even hotter when your cheeks get all pink like that." One side of his mouth rose in a slight smile and she wondered how she could be so warm when there was still snow on parts of the ground.

"I guess I'm not accustomed to people giving me compliments about…about something that doesn't involve my horses or my business."

"Probably because they're too afraid to get shot down."

"Why?"

Dylan shrugged, but his expression remained confident. "I guess some men get intimidated by a smart and beautiful woman."

Okay, he needed to stop with all this talk about her appearance. It was getting her all flustered and she was having a hard time concentrating on the conversation. "No, I meant why would I shoot them down?"

"Do you?"

"Do I what?" Her lips parted in confusion.

"Shoot a guy down when he asks you out?"

Robin snapped her mouth shut. She couldn't very well admit that she didn't get asked out very often. Focusing on a spot behind him, she asked, "Are we talking about my dating life or about your house remodel?"

He crossed his arms as he leaned back to give her a full appraisal. "I'd like to talk about both, but I suppose one of those topics isn't any of my business."

If she were good at flirting, this would be the time to tell him that she wanted to make her dating life his business. But what if it came out sounding desperate? Or worse, what if he told her that he already had more business than he could handle? Instead of humiliating herself any further, she drew in a long breath. "Listen, Dylan, I'm not the type of woman you consult for decorating tips. I'm more the type that you would ask to accompany you to the feedstore. Or a livestock auction."

He narrowed only one eye, almost giving him the appearance of winking. "How are you in a tractor supply setting?"

She extended her arm in a wide arc as though to say, *There you go. Now you're getting it.* "I can hold my own."

"Perfect. There's a tractor supply place on the way to the home improvement warehouse in Wonderstone Ridge. On Thursday, we can swing by the feedstore and then hit that livestock auction at the Bronco Convention Center on Saturday."

"Wait. What?" Robin scratched her head, knocking her ponytail off-center. Although, now it matched the rest of her, which was feeling equally off-center.

"Assuming that would work with your schedule." Dylan pulled out his phone and swiped until he opened the calendar app. "I can't leave until two tomorrow since Mickie is coming in for her first day and I'll need to walk her through some things."

Robin lost all ability to protest, or even respond with much more than a nod of her head as she pulled out her own phone to accept his calendar invite. It all happened so fast. Before she knew it, Dylan was telling her he had to get going to his next meeting and thanking her for all her help today.

If Robin had been slightly in awe when the plumber

had driven away earlier, she was in complete shock by the time she got inside her own truck to leave. Dylan Sanchez was truly a smooth talker. How had a simple offer of advice yesterday turned into several hours and two meals with the man today, and then the promise of at least three dates later this week?

No, they weren't dates, she told herself as she pulled onto the long dirt driveway better known as Broken Road. They were shopping trips. Shopping trips that would benefit his ranch. That would benefit him.

Although, if she was being honest, they would also benefit her because it meant she'd get to spend more time with Dylan. And wasn't that her goal? Why she'd even considered entering the bake-off in the first place? If she was going to use her feminine wiles—or lack thereof—to get close to a man, she was going to have better luck if she was on familiar territory. She'd definitely be more comfortable inside a feedstore rather than baking cookies in the kitchen.

Still. None of this was going quite how she'd envisioned. Her plan had taken an unexpected turn, and something wasn't sitting right. Maybe it was the fact that Robin had formulated a plan in the first place instead of allowing nature to take its course. In her defense, though, her entire business model for her line of horse therapeutic products was based on the premise that sometimes nature needed a little help moving things along.

Except her products were designed to benefit the horse in the long run. When it came to her crush on Dylan Sanchez, Robin wasn't sure who was benefiting from her plan. Was she using his ranch as an excuse to get close to him? Or was he using her to get closer to his goal of having a successful ranch?

An unease settled over her as she drove to Cimarron Rose to check on a capsule collection of mane products she'd developed for the Rein Rejuvenation's grooming line. For years she'd dedicated herself to growing her business, and throwing herself into her work was always a default when she wanted to avoid anything uncomfortable.

But the discomforting doubt didn't go away at the boutique owned by Evy, her cousin Wes's wife, and only grew stronger by the time she returned home. That evening, Robin reached for her phone multiple times to call Dylan and tell him that she couldn't go to the home improvement store. However, as soon as her finger would hover over the screen, she couldn't make herself tap that green button. She needed just a few more hours with him before she could convince herself that she was wasting her time. Plus, there was a small part of her that was flattered he'd wanted her opinion. She went back and forth in her head until right before eleven o'clock on Wednesday morning when her phone pinged with a text notification.

When she saw Dylan's name, Robin's heart picked up speed. Her brain quickly shut down any excitement. He was probably sending her a message to cancel. Feeling foolish for not canceling first, she sighed as she opened the text.

Mickie has already made herself comfortable and politely suggested I "get lost" so she can set things up the way she wants. Dylan included a photo of a no-nonsense-looking older woman sorting papers behind the reception area desk. A second message popped up below. I know we agreed on 2:00, but is there any chance you can slip away sooner? I can pick you up.

Robin's pulse skyrocketed again, and she took three breaths in quick succession to get ahold of herself. This was *not* a date. At least not in his mind. He was simply asking her to tag along with him and give him some advice.

If she was going to help Dylan, then she should really help him by giving him a sneak peek into what he was getting himself into. A sudden idea occurred to her, and she quickly typed a response.

If you can make it to the Bonnie B in the next hour, you'll find me in the cowshed on the south side of the property.

Smiling to herself, she shoved her phone into her back pocket. Then she told the cow in the stall with her, "Let's see how Mr. Smooth Talker does on an actual working ranch."

## Chapter Five

Dylan knew a setup when he walked straight into one.

Because if Robin would've told him that he was going to find her inside a stall with another ranch hand and a bleating cow about to give birth, there was no way Dylan would have raced across town to get to the Bonnie B.

"You ready to witness something incredible?" she asked, her eyes radiating the same excitement in her tone. She looked so wholesome and completely in her element, the same attraction he'd experienced yesterday returned like a swift kick to his gut.

"Can I witness it from this side of the stall?" Dylan asked. He'd owned his own ranch for a couple of months now and was used to the smell of manure. But the scent of amniotic fluid spilled on fresh straw hit the nostrils differently. "I don't want to make the mother-to-be nervous."

"This is Becky's fourth birth. A pro like her doesn't get nervous anymore." In response, Becky made a whimpering moo. "But she's definitely in pain, aren't you, girl?"

Robin remained by the cow's head, murmuring words of encouragement as the ranch hand knelt behind Becky, ready to help guide the calf out. Yep, this was definitely different than when Princess had her litter of puppies. And despite his initial hesitation, Dylan was so completely mesmerized by the process that he didn't look away once.

"You got this, girl." Dylan followed Robin's lead, wanting to offer the cow some verbal motivation. Although, perhaps he wasn't quite as calm as the labor progressed and he continued to cheer from the sidelines. "There are the front hooves, and the head. It's time to bring it on home, Becky. Okay, that last contraction was a swing and a miss, but you're going to get it on the next one."

A burst of adrenaline pumped through his body when the calf was safely delivered, making him feel as though he'd just hit a home run, scored a touchdown and made a three-pointer all in one. Dylan whooped and lifted his arms in victory. "Way to knock it out of the park, Becky!"

The ranch hand paused his examination of the newborn to tilt his head in Dylan's direction. Dylan immediately lowered his voice. "Sorry, I'm used to coaching youth sports and got a little excited there for a second."

Robin bit her lower lip as she came out of the stall, leaving the exhausted cow to bond with her calf. Dylan caught the twinkle of something in the woman's eyes.

"That was incredible," he said, then looked around at the surrounding pens holding very pregnant cows. "You have any other ones in labor we can watch?"

Robin let loose with the laugh she'd apparently been holding back. When she finished, she shook her head. "It's still early in the birthing season, but if you come back in March, we average about two or three a day. I have to admit, this isn't exactly the response I was expecting from you."

"I wasn't expecting it from myself, either. I had my doubts at first, but then something came over me and the whole experience seemed so natural, so right. I think I can actually do this, Robin."

"They're not always this easy," Robin warned. "The heifers are first timers and not all of them are as calm as Becky. They might not respond as well to your shouts about sticking with the hard-court press and staying loose."

"They will if I install some TVs in the barn so they can watch the sports channels."

"So you're really committing to this, huh?" Robin's smile was wide. "You're going to breed cattle?"

"Why? Was this some sort of test?" Dylan looked at the cow, who was already back on her feet and licking her calf clean. "Were you in on this, too, Becky?"

"Yes, Becky was the mastermind." The cow mooed her agreement and Robin gave Dylan's arm a playful shove. "See. She says you passed. I need to go wash up and change before we go. Do you want to stay here or follow me over to the main house?"

Dylan had passed the massive home on his way to the barn area. He was curious if the inside was just as spectacular as the wood beam and river rock architecture outside suggested. He'd once gone to Jordan Taylor's equally impressive family home for his sister's rehearsal dinner and had been disappointed to discover that something so beautiful could also be utterly devoid of warmth. At the time, his curiosity about how the other half lived had only made him feel more like an outsider.

Dylan wasn't ready to feel that way with Robin. Yet.

"Actually, I'll just cruise around the maternity ward here and see if any of the ladies need me to give them a pep talk."

"Okay, Coach," Robin said. "I'll meet you outside in ten minutes."

There were several employees hard at work and he didn't want to bother them with questions. Although he did have plenty of questions. Instead, Dylan walked around the pens taking mental notes before heading outside. It would require a lot more people and a hell of a lot more money to get his operation up to this level. After his rec league game last night, he'd buried himself in research about the pros and cons of breeding cattle as well as the expected profit margins. He'd learned that bigger ranches, like the Bonnie B, had the resources to both breed and raise their own cattle. But a ranch the size of his was better suited to doing one or the other. He'd been a little late to the party figuring out the differences, but at least he had a better sense of direction now, thanks to Robin.

As he stood outside one of several cowsheds, comparing the size of the structure to his own barn, a man in his sixties called out to him. "Hey, Dylan, what brings you out to the Bonnie B? Is there a problem with one of the new trucks?"

"Hi, Mr. Abernathy." Dylan lifted his hand in greeting. Robin must've gotten her height and blond hair from her father, but that was where the resemblance ended. No wonder he hadn't recognized her that day at the dealership. "I'm not here on business. Or at least not on car business. I'm waiting for Robin. She's helping me with a project out at my ranch."

Just saying the words *my ranch* to such a respected member of the Bronco community gave Dylan a thrill of satisfaction.

"Right. I heard you and Hank Hardy worked out a pretty sweet deal for Broken Road Ranch."

*Sweet deal.* See? Even Asa Abernathy saw that Dylan had made a smart investment. His chest swelled with pride. "We did."

"Also heard he left the place a mess. Old Hank was never cut out for the ranching life."

Some of Dylan's confidence took a slight dip. The last thing he wanted was for anyone to say those same words about him. Many of the people in this town possibly thought it, and might even talk about it amongst themselves. They wouldn't for long, though. Dylan would prove all the doubters wrong, but not by comparing himself to Hank. And definitely not by complaining that his ranch was anything less than what he hoped it would be. He recovered by pushing his shoulders back and smiling anyway. Sometimes, a guy had to hard-sell himself. Other times, the best response was no response.

Asa Abernathy seemed like the type of person who could tell when someone was feeding him a line. Dylan's gamble to wait it out worked because the man continued. "Anyway, if Robin's getting you squared away then you shouldn't have any problems."

"That's what I'm hoping, sir." Dylan appreciated the man's faith in his daughter. After all, his own parents weren't shy about singing their children's praises. The Abernathys might be wealthy, but at least they weren't as stuffy as the Taylor patriarchs.

"Although, if I'm being honest." Mr. Abernathy leaned in closer but didn't bother to lower his voice. "I wish my little girl would stop getting caught up in all these hobbies and start thinking more about her future."

"I think about my future all the time, Dad." Robin joined the conversation before Dylan had even noticed her walk up. And before he had time to wonder if Mr. Abernathy was referring to him and the Broken Road Ranch as one of his daughter's hobbies. "For the record, Rein Rejuvenation isn't a hobby. The CPA said my income last year was almost on pace to match my trust dividends."

Dylan tried not to wince. Of course Robin had a

trust account. It was another reminder that unlike him, she didn't have anything to prove financially.

"What happened to your mouth?" her father asked, drawing Dylan's attention from Robin's snug jeans to her lips, which were much redder than they'd been when she'd left the barn. "Did Becky whip you with her tail again? Or is that from the dye you've been using in those practice cookies?"

"No, Dad." Robin's cheeks were getting close to matching the shade of her lips. "It's just lipstick."

"Since when do you wear—" Mr. Abernathy must have read something in his daughter's glare because he wisely stopped talking and faced Dylan. "Anyway, where are you two off to?"

"I have to go to a home improvement wholesaler in Wonderstone Ridge and we're going to stop by Turner's Tractor Supply either on the way there or on the way back."

"On the way there," Robin corrected. "They close at five and we probably won't be done looking at bathroom vanities by then."

"Whoa." Dylan held up both palms. "Nobody mentioned anything about vanities. I thought it was just the toilets and shower tile getting redone."

Robin pushed a loose strand of hair away from her face. "That makes no sense. Why would you update most of the room, yet leave those old rotting cabinets in there?"

Dylan started to respond, but Mr. Abernathy made a tsking sound. "Son, it's better to just follow along when she gets going in a certain direction. Did she tell you that her brothers call her Trail Boss?"

Robin rolled her eyes. "I'm not bossy. I'm practical."

"Sure, honey. Let's go with that. When you're at the tractor supply store, will you ask Johnny Lee when they're expecting their next shipment of electric cultivators? Your mother is talking about replanting her garden."

"Not the gardening idea again. Remember when she forgot about those tomato plants a few years ago and we had that rabbit infestation?"

"You know how your mother is. She needs a project just like—" Her father stopped, making Dylan think the man knew better than to refer to Robin's penchant for projects again.

"But she has baby Frankie to dote on now," Robin pointed out. Dylan knew firefighter Jace Abernathy had adopted a baby boy after assisting with the birth during an emergency call. In fact, Robin's brother had also helped deliver Dylan's niece Merry. He was pretty sure that Jace and his fiancée, Tamara, now lived in their own house out here on the Bonnie B with their baby.

"Speaking of grandchildren," her father continued as he hooked his thumbs through his belt loops, "now that Billy's kids are getting older, your mom thinks Frankie needs some cousins his own age. So unless you want her focusing on which one of our children is going to provide the next baby, I suggest you let her run with her gardening project."

"That sounds familiar," Dylan mumbled to himself, but apparently his words were louder than he'd meant them to be.

"What's that?" Mr. Abernathy asked.

Dylan cleared his throat. "Mrs. Abernathy sounds like my parents. My niece is only two months old and already my mom and dad are dropping hints about more grandchildren."

"Is that right?" Mr. Abernathy studied Dylan rather intently, looking him over from head to toe.

Dylan's eyes shot to Robin, hoping she could explain why her dad was suddenly sizing him up like a prized bull. But Robin's expression looked equally confused. Or mortified. He couldn't tell which.

"Okay, Dad, we have to get going." Robin grabbed Dylan's arm and tugged him toward the truck. Although, she didn't have to use too much force because he was eager to get away from what had suddenly become a tricky conversation.

"You two have fun," Mr. Abernathy called. Dylan could feel the man staring at their retreating backs, so he only turned around long enough to give a quick wave goodbye. Something inspired Mr. Abernathy to give another parting comment. "And take your time. Maybe grab a bite to eat while you're there. Robin is less bossy when she's eating."

Robin gasped as her head pivoted to give her dad another warning look, reminding Dylan of the same expression his sisters used whenever someone in their family embarrassed them. He would've laughed, but since Robin was too busy silently communicating her displeasure at her father behind them, she didn't see the icy patch in front of her. The hand she'd been using to propel Dylan forward was still on his arm when she slipped, making her close enough for him to catch before she stumbled.

Even though she'd quickly regained her footing, he slid his arm around her, allowing his palm to curve along her small waist. Surprised brown eyes locked onto his, her thick lashes fluttering at him several times. "S-sorry. I wasn't watching where I was going."

"Good catch, Dylan." Mr. Abernathy was apparently still keeping tabs on them, which for some reason made Dylan want to prove that he was more than capable of continuing to protect her.

Hauling her against his side, Dylan steered Robin toward a melted spot on the road and kept his arm firmly in place as he walked her to his truck. Man, she fit so perfectly beside him, he was reluctant to let her go. If her dad hadn't been there, Dylan might not have.

"Please ignore everything my father just said and did," Robin said under her breath when Dylan opened the passenger door for her. "And for the record, I'm not that bossy."

"You kind of are," Dylan replied. When she opened her mouth to object, he added, "I do like your red lips, though."

Robin thought she'd been subtle borrowing her sister Stacy's lipstick. And then her dad had gone and pointed it out right in front of Dylan.

If that hadn't been embarrassing enough, her father had taken things one step further by mentioning grandchildren and then suggesting Robin and Dylan have dinner together. When it came to playing matchmaker, Asa Abernathy clearly had more experience pairing livestock than humans.

Robin had been in such a hurry to get away from her father's mortifying comments that she would have fallen flat on her face if Dylan hadn't been there to catch her. Then she'd been so stunned by the feel of his hand above her hip that she'd allowed herself to believe that his gentlemanly attention made this outing almost seem like a date.

Even though she knew it wasn't.

When Dylan made that comment about liking her lipstick, though, Robin couldn't think of anything but the way he was staring at her mouth as he said it. Not knowing how to respond, especially with her father still a few yards away and pretending like he wasn't watching them, Robin panicked and launched herself inside his truck. Hastily, she reached for the interior handle and almost caught Dylan's elbow with the edge of the door when she slammed it shut in his face.

She took several deep breaths as he made his way to the driver's side, warning herself not to look in the sideview mirror for fear of seeing exactly how red her face was. In fact, she took her time pretending to be absorbed in the process of securing her seat belt so that she wouldn't have to make eye contact with him.

However, she didn't have to be looking in his direction to see that he was removing an item of clothing. She inhaled the passing scent of his cologne as he tossed his jacket over the armrest and into the back seat.

Oh boy. Now she had to risk taking a peek. Her mouth went dry. Unlike the normal button-up shirts she'd seen him wear for work, he had on a snug-fitting Henley that showed every ridge of his athletic muscles underneath.

Great. How was she supposed to keep her cool when the man looked and smelled this good?

Luckily, Dylan got a phone call just as he started the truck. "Do you mind if I take this?"

"By all means," she said, relieved to have a few more moments to regain her composure.

He answered before shifting into gear. As much as Robin tried not to pay attention, it was hard to ignore since he was using the speakerphone and the caller's voice was broadcast throughout the cab of the truck.

"Dylan, it's Keith Monk from the Helena dealership. I have a customer here who is interested in the crossover SUV sport but only if she can get it in Carefree Crimson. I don't have one in that color, but was looking at the inventory database online and saw that you might. I called your office hoping you still have yours in stock, but some woman answered the phone."

"Yes, that's Mickie." Dylan looked both ways before pulling out onto the highway. "She's my new office manager."

"Well, she said that you guys have to hold on to all your red inventory for some sort of baking contest you're having. Something about a Valentine's Day color scheme. What's that all about?"

Dylan muttered a curse under his breath. "You have any sisters, Keith?"

"Can't say that I do."

"Then it'll be too hard for me to explain." Without going into any more detail, Dylan went on to negotiate a swap with Keith, telling the salesman he could send the red SUV and a blue sedan in exchange for a pair of red convertibles and a white minivan.

Even though they were using several acronyms and other terms Robin didn't understand, Dylan's voice was confident and leisurely and almost soothing. It wasn't long before the tension in her muscles had completely vanished, and she relaxed into the heated leather seat.

When the deal was made and delivery coordinated, Keith again asked, "So what's going on with the cooking show?"

"It's a bake-off. I'll email you the flyer if you're interested in signing up." Dylan said goodbye and disconnected before apologizing to Robin. "Sorry about that."

"Business comes first," Robin said, reminding herself, as well. It wasn't like he'd taken a call while they were on an actual date. "So you're going to decorate your entire parking lot with red and white cars for Valentine's Day?"

"I have no idea. Obviously, Camilla and Sofia already told Mickie their plans before they bothered to fill me in. Probably because they knew I would've put my foot down."

"I've met both of your sisters and I think it's cute that you're under the impression you could actually put your foot down with them."

"I put my foot down all the time."

"Like when?" Robin asked. "Give me an example."

"Like the time Sofia wanted me to wear a pink shirt in some fundraiser fashion show at the boutique where she works."

"You were in a fashion show at BH Couture? Like as a model?"

"Yes." He pointed one finger. "But not in that shirt. Why? You don't think I could be a model?"

"On the contrary. I think a lot of women—and men—would buy whatever you were selling." But mostly women. Dylan had a reputation for being a carefree and charismatic bachelor and Robin had a feeling it was well-earned. "So you draw the line at wearing pink. What else?"

"Oh, I'm fine with wearing pink. It was more the cut of the shirt and how it felt on my arms. I hate constricting fabric. I need to be able to move." He extended and retracted his forearm in a way that caused his bicep to flex under the soft material of his current shirt. Suddenly Robin needed to take off her own jacket. "I also put my foot down when it comes to my turn to cook Sunday dinner. Nobody ever wants to do appetizer night except Dante, so my family always tries to get me to try something besides buffalo wings and nachos. You want me to let you in on a little secret?"

Robin got butterflies in her tummy every time Dylan lowered his voice that way. "Sure."

"You know the flaming fajitas incident everybody in town seems to have heard about?"

Robin recalled mentioning it to him the day they met. "Of course."

"It was totally worth singeing off my eyebrows and being the subject of everyone's jokes for three whole weeks because now my family lets me cook whatever I want. As long as open flames aren't involved."

Was there anything sexier than a man who could laugh at himself? Robin didn't think so. Unless it was the matching dimples in Dylan's cheeks when he did laugh.

Before she could fall completely under his spell, Robin challenged, "I don't know if a cooking mishap that you didn't plan counts as putting your foot down."

"Fair enough. Then how about the time Camilla and Jordan tried to pay for my parents' kitchen remodel. I insisted on matching whatever amount they were contributing. Which is a good thing because now I know what I'm getting into with the cost of materials and the labor delays. Although, it's also a bad thing because now Camilla expects me to know how great of a deal her restaurant equipment supplier is getting me for the rental of a bunch of commercial-grade ovens. Which reminds me, I need to figure out which part of the lot she plans to use for them."

"The ovens are for the bake-off?" Robin no longer had to worry about being too flushed because her blood went cold.

"Yeah." Dylan pulled ahead of an 18-wheeler and picked up speed.

"You're holding the bake-off at the dealership? As in contestants are going to make their recipes all together? In the middle of an open parking lot?"

"Someone mentioned some heated party tents, but the idea was to generate some extra money and every time I turn around, it seems like my family is spending more of it."

Crap. Robin hadn't realized that she would actually have to bake her cookies in front of witnesses. She needed to figure out a way to back out of this contest, but without seeming like she was afraid of coming in last place. Was it too much to hope for a blizzard to cancel the entire thing?

"So if you don't want to do the bake-off and you don't like the idea of having red and white cars on your lot during it, then why aren't you putting your foot down for this?" Robin asked. "I mean, as far as risks go, I'd be more concerned about having control over a business promotion than I'd be about a tight shirt making my biceps look amazing."

Unfortunately, they were on a long stretch of road with no oncoming traffic and he felt safe enough to tilt his head as he looked directly at her. "You think my biceps look amazing?"

"Keep your eyes on the road," she said, refusing to answer a question he surely knew the answer to already. "And tell me why you're letting your sisters have free rein when you clearly want nothing to do with this contest."

"Because I love my family and it makes my mom and sisters happy to feel like they're helping me. Plus, as much as I hate the entire concept, I also trust them to pull it off. I have no idea how they'll manage it, but if anyone can make something work, it's them."

Robin looked out the window, blinking several times to clear the dampness from her eyes. If she thought it was attractive that Dylan could poke fun at himself, she was absolutely impressed—and touched—by his ability to speak so highly of the women in his life. Her dad always said that it would take a confident man to not be intimidated by his strong-willed daughter.

And Dylan Sanchez was definitely not intimidated by strong women.

But then again, he'd never been to a tractor supply store with Robin Abernathy.

She'd learned to drive a John Deere 6 Series before she'd been allowed to drive a car and was usually the first person to hop in the cab when a row of alfalfa needed to be tilled or an irrigation channel needed to be cleared. If only she could be as confident about her expertise in baking cookies as she was with horses and farm equipment.

When they pulled into the lot of Turner's, a place she'd been coming to since before she could walk, Robin realized that she'd never asked him why they were going there in the first place. They'd talked

about his barn layout, his fencing, even his fertilizer needs. But they'd never talked about heavy ma-
chinery.

"Do you know what you're looking for here?" she
asked.

"I think so," Dylan replied. "But I'm sure you'll
let me know if I get something wrong."

He winked at her, just like she'd winked at him the
other day to let him know that she wouldn't tell Brad
she'd figured out the plumbing issue before he had.
Was this going to be another instance of her having to
jump in to explain something to Dylan? Because no
matter how confident he was around strong women,
she wasn't looking forward to living up to her Trail
Boss nickname. Again.

But it turned out that Dylan knew exactly what he
wanted. And it wasn't a brand-new tractor. Robin's
jaw nearly fell open when he told the man who greeted
them, "I've got an International Harvester 856 that
needs a new clutch, water pump gasket and a set of
brake piston O-rings."

Johnny Lee Turner, the owner, asked about the
year and horsepower and Dylan easily rattled off details that helped the older man locate the parts that
would fit. Robin was left to follow behind as she
silently stared in amazement at Dylan's knowledge
about something ranch related.

"What about tires?" Johnny Lee asked as they
passed a display of wheels.

"I already had my service tech order some from
my wholesale dealer. Speaking of which, how's your

wife liking her new wagon? Has she noticed a difference having the all-wheel drive with the snow?"

Of course. Robin nearly slapped her forehead at the late realization. No wonder Dylan was so comfortable talking shop about tractors. He was a car guy and engines were engines. When Johnny Lee finished gushing about how much his wife was enjoying her new car from, not surprisingly, Bronco Motors, Robin finally spoke up.

"Wait, how much are the tires from your wholesale person, Dylan?"

Dylan relayed an amount that was significantly cheaper than the price tag above the display in front of them.

"Hmm…" Robin tapped her chin. "So then why does the Bonnie B pay so much for tires?"

Johnny Lee squinted, then pushed his glasses higher on his bulbous nose. "Is that you, Lil' Robin Abernathy? I didn't recognize you with your hair down like that and all that makeup."

Her fingers flew to her mouth. Why was everyone acting like she'd just undergone some drastic makeover? Was she normally so hideous looking that a simple swipe of lipstick made that much of a difference? Refusing to be distracted, though, she squared her shoulders and lifted an eyebrow, waiting for him to answer her original question.

"Now I know what you're thinking, Lil' Robin," Johnny Lee said. For some reason, his tone sounded a bit more condescending. Probably because he referred to her by the same name he'd been calling her since she was three years old. "But the markup is on account of me having to pay added delivery fees plus the cost of keeping so many tires in stock. That way, they're readily available as soon as you need them."

"Yeah, I know how retail prices work, Johnny Lee, and the concept of supply and demand." After all, Robin was a business owner, as well. "But our ranch goes through a lot of tires and I'm wondering if it would be more cost-efficient for us to just deal directly with Dylan's wholesaler."

"I don't know if Mario will give you the same prices he gives me," Dylan said, then shrugged. "But I guess it wouldn't hurt to ask him."

"Why wouldn't he give me the same price?" Robin asked. Was he part of some good ol' boy network that only did business with men? She was certainly starting to get that impression from Johnny Lee.

"Because you didn't help him with his econ homework in college, and you don't volunteer to coach his son's Little League team with him."

"Humph." She crossed her arms in front of her chest, somewhat defeated. "I could comp him some horse therapeutic products."

"He doesn't have a horse."

Robin tried to think of something else she could bargain with. "What about a few hundred pounds of grass fed beef?"

"He's vegan."

Johnny Lee gasped. "And this tire friend of yours lives here in Montana?"

"Born and raised," Dylan confirmed, clearly holding back a smirk.

Robin's friend Daphne Taylor had caused quite a stir within her family when she'd announced to her ranching father that she no longer ate meat and was opening an animal sanctuary. Some of the old-timers in town were still adapting to the current century.

"I don't know that your daddy would want to buy tires from some granola-eating type, Lil' Robin. Best you just keep getting them here at Turner's. I got me a big freezer at home that could fit a whole rack of beef if you wanted to work out some sort of trade."

Robin frowned at the older man's offer, which frankly, was a little late considering they'd been paying full price all these years.

"Actually, Johnny Lee," Dylan said as he flashed that same smile he'd used yesterday with Brad the plumber, "Mrs. Abernathy was hoping to get a top-of-the-line electric cultivator for her garden. Why don't you let Robin take that one home with her today. I think it would go a long way in sweetening the pot when she tells her father about your generous offer to discount the Bonnie B's tires by 20 percent."

Robin's eyes widened at Dylan's audacity, but she kept her mouth closed as the owner seemed to actually be considering his suggestion. She'd also completely forgotten about her mom's cultivator, so she was amazed Dylan had remembered. But more than that, she was both impressed and slightly aroused by his negotiation skills.

When Dylan loaded the cultivator into the bed of

his truck ten minutes later, Robin realized that this little crush she'd developed was going to turn out to be a bigger problem if she ended up like everyone else in this town and couldn't resist his charm.

## Chapter Six

Robin stared reluctantly at the entrance to the home improvement warehouse and asked, "Are you sure we should be doing this before we eat?"

Dylan looked at his watch. "Maybe you're right. It's already five o'clock and I only had a protein bar for lunch. There's a taco shop across the street, unless you had your mind set on eating somewhere fancier?"

Was she expecting him to take her to a five-star restaurant while they were out running errands? No. Did she hope they could possibly go somewhere a little more romantic than a fluorescent-lit fast-food joint in a strip mall? Maybe.

Unfortunately, her dad was right and Robin was more feisty when she was hungry. Or overwhelmed with cabinet choices. She didn't want to scare off Dylan by having their first major argument in front of a display of toilets. Still, she was a little defensive when she asked, "Why would I expect fancier? Did you think I was the prissy type?"

"Not when I watched you chow down that double bacon cheeseburger yesterday. But then today I saw the house where you grew up and realized that you may be accustomed to something a little more formal."

His comment gave her pause. As a kid, she'd been aware that her home was bigger than some of the others in town. By the time she was in high school, the financial disparity between her and her classmates became more noticeable and she realized that some people treated her differently when they found out her last name was Abernathy. It wasn't until her second date with an ambitious rodeo cowboy when she was twenty-two that she realized there were men out there who were only interested in her because of her family's bank account. She really hoped Dylan wasn't the same way.

"Formal?" She pushed her hair back, still not used to having it down around her shoulders. "Did I look formal when I was covered with straw and amniotic fluid back in the cowshed?"

"No, but then you got all dressed up."

Her arms dropped quickly to her sides, causing her palms to slap her hips. "I'm wearing lipstick. That's the only difference. Why is everyone acting as though I transformed into some sort of alien from outer space?"

"It's not that. It's just that those jeans are a lot tighter and the sweater under your jacket is…uh…

the neckline is just a little more…" His hands made a V symbol in front of his own chest.

She glanced down and saw that the wide opening of her sweater dipped low enough to expose the curve of her breasts. She jerked the lapels of her jacket closed. "I borrowed this from my sister's closet. I guess I should've worn a shirt underneath it."

"I think it looks great exactly the way you have it." Dylan's dimples were now in full effect.

Her legs trembled slightly, and she didn't think it was from the new knee-high boots her mom had just bought her.

"So tacos sound good, yeah?" Robin said a bit too quickly before starting out across the parking lot. Luckily, Dylan caught up to her and didn't say anything else until after they'd ordered their food.

"I don't think the cashier was expecting you to speak such perfect Spanish," Dylan said as Robin filled a plastic cup with hot carrots and jalapeños from the salsa bar.

"I did a semester abroad in Argentina with my equestrian studies program and nobody down there seemed to think anything of a blonde American speaking Spanish. But here in Montana, it always catches people off guard."

"Probably because your accent is almost as good as mine. And my dad and Uncle Stanley are originally from Mexico, so I grew up speaking it."

"*Almost* as good?" Robin lifted her chin and challenged, "Let me hear it."

If she thought Dylan's voice had been soothing

when he'd been on the phone earlier talking about mundane things such as factory incentives and cruise control options, it was absolute magic when he spoke to her in Spanish. She hadn't realized she'd closed her eyes listening to him until he said, *"Tu comprende?"*

"What?" She blinked several times. "Yes, of course I understand. You said that you know white marble countertops are classy and expensive, but you always wanted butcher-block countertops because your aunt Celia, Uncle Stanley's late wife, had them in her kitchen and used to make the best tortillas on them. So they remind you of home-cooked food."

"For a second there, I thought I might be boring you. Any other languages you speak?"

Robin shook her head. "Nope. But we did have a ranch hand once from Germany who taught me and my siblings some bad words."

Dylan repeated the same curses, making Robin laugh.

"Wait. What other languages do *you* speak?"

"French, Mandarin and Arabic. And one of the salespeople at the dealership is really into K-pop, so I can sing a few verses in Korean, but I have no idea what they mean."

Robin's jaw went slack, again taken by surprise. He must've been accustomed to the response—or at least expected it—because he shrugged. "I was an international business major in college. At one time, I planned to make my fortune in the global stock exchanges, but it turns out I liked living in Bronco too much to ever move overseas."

"So you became a car salesman instead?" she asked.

Dylan shrugged. "It was supposed to be a summer job, but one commission led to another and before I knew it, I got the opportunity to open my own dealership. I like cars almost as much as sports and since there isn't a high demand for a professional basketball franchise in Bronco, I found something I could do that I was decent at."

The person behind the counter called their order number. Robin watched with a new sense of wonder as Dylan walked across the restaurant to retrieve their food. He was a great salesman and obviously well educated. But like her, he also had a close family and deep roots in their small town. He'd even mentioned before that his desire to make money was more of a means to an end. His real dream was to own his own land.

Leaning back comfortably in her chair, she was more certain than ever that she'd made the right decision to assist him in making his dream a reality.

At least she was until they finished eating and were crossing the street heading back toward the home improvement warehouse again.

Robin's pace slowed. "I was just thinking that your sister Sofia is in the fashion industry. Camilla owns a restaurant and is probably an expert on kitchen layouts. And Eloise has impeccable taste. Don't you think you should've brought one of them to help you pick stuff out for your new home?"

"Maybe. But you volunteered." He continued walking toward the entrance.

"I didn't exactly volunteer for this part," she pointed out. Her words failed to slow him down.

In fact, it felt as though he was now moving faster. "Except you kind of did."

"But, Dylan, home improvement is such a personal thing. You're going to have to live in the house once it's done. Not me. What if you don't like something I pick out?"

"Then I'll tell you that I don't like it. I'm not afraid to put my foot down with you, too, Robin. Just like I'm currently refusing to let you talk your way out of this."

He must've realized that she wasn't following him, because he turned around and grasped her hand to pull her along. His grip was firm but gentle and radiated heat all the way up her arm and into her chest. For someone whose nickname was Trail Boss, she certainly had no problem allowing him to lead her. This was the second time today he'd physically taken control of a situation and somehow it made her feel more secure.

He didn't let go of her hand, even when they stepped inside. The vastness of the store caused her to inch closer to him. As if staying glued to his side wouldn't make the shopping trip quite so overwhelming. "There's certainly a lot more options here than at the hardware store in town."

"I know. I hate not buying locally, but Brad said he could get everything for a much lower price here with his contractor's license. He also said we only need to take pictures of what we want and send them to him. He'll come back and pick up the items."

"Do we have a list of everything we'll...*you'll* need?" Robin knew she'd been guilty of using the *we* word yesterday. But that was back when she'd been trying to get Dylan to agree to her ideas by appealing to his sports team mentality. Now, she was questioning if that had been the best approach since her original plan seemed to be moving so quickly.

"Brad emailed it to me this morning." Dylan paused in front of a row of bathtubs. "Mickie was working on a spreadsheet with all the contact info for the bake-off contestants, so I asked if she had your email address on there. She found it and said she'd forward you the list. Check your inbox."

Robin reluctantly released his hand to pull out her phone. Sure enough, there was an email from Dylan's new office manager. But a thought popped into Robin's mind before she could read it. "So Mickie knows we're here together?"

"Yeah, why wouldn't she?"

"Does anyone else know?"

"Besides your dad, my brother Dante, who is in the middle of his own remodel project with Eloise, and probably my sisters and parents. Oh, and also Brad and everyone else on our rec basketball team since we all went to Doug's bar together last night after the game. I'm not sure who else might know. Why? Is it supposed to be a secret that we're hanging out?"

*Okay. Keep breathing normally and don't freak out.* This was no big deal. So what if Dylan just told a bunch of people at the town bar that he was "hanging out" with her? He hung out with a lot of women, from the sounds of things. There'd always been the risk that people would eventually figure out Robin had a crush on him. She just wasn't ready yet for the public humiliation if he ended up rejecting her.

"Nope. No secret on my end." Robin made her voice sound as casual as possible, trying to focus her attention on the emailed list. Although she couldn't help but ask, "Um, did anyone say anything about it?"

Dylan pulled out a tape measure she didn't know he had and stretched it out across one of the bathtubs. "About us hanging out?"

"Yeah." Robin continued to pretend as though she were completely engrossed in reading the words floating around the screen in front of her.

"What would they say?"

Oh, what *wouldn't* they say? But Robin didn't voice that thought aloud, probably because she didn't want to really hear the answer. Bronco was a small town and small towns meant big gossip. And gossip wasn't always complimentary. But then again, she was merely helping Dylan on his ranch. It wasn't as though people would immediately jump to the conclusion that they were dating. Because they clearly weren't.

"This is a nice tub," Robin said, changing the subject and hoping he didn't notice her internal distress about their nonrelationship. "I like the gold claw feet on the bottom. It makes it look like an antique, but it's much bigger than the old-fashioned ones."

"I was thinking the same thing," he said. "I'm not really a bath guy, but if I'm going to buy one, I want to at least fit in it."

Robin drew in a ragged breath at the mental image of Dylan Sanchez soaking in the tub, his hair wet and his chest bare… She cleared her throat. "What about the faucet? Would you do something in a gold color to match the feet?"

And that's how it went for the next hour. Sinks, mirrors, vanities, it was like something clicked between them and they both liked the exact same things because they were making quick work of their list. He'd pick a tile for the backsplash, and she'd suggest a lighting fixture. Then they'd both nod their heads and move on to the next item. She'd stop to look at a hardwood floor sample and he'd take a picture and type in the item number and price. Check. The kitchen was a no-brainer because she already knew what kind of countertops he wanted and they both loved the blue cabinets, even though they'd have to be custom ordered. They even pointed to the same drawer pulls at the same moment. The only time they weren't in complete agreement was when he thought the window shutters were the next aisle over and she thought they'd already passed them. They'd both been wrong.

Before Robin knew it, they were done. She shoved her phone in her back pocket. "That was way easier than I thought it would be."

"I know." Dylan looked around the store at several other people, including three couples, who seemed to be in the same sections they'd started in. "It feels like we should get some sort of prize for finishing so quickly."

"Like a double fudge brownie sundae?"

"From Cubby's?"

"I mean, it is on the way home," Robin said, wishing it wasn't already time for them to leave.

But Rome—and Broken Road Ranch—wasn't be built in a day. For the first time in Robin Abernathy's life, she would just have to be patient.

"Why haven't you responded to any messages in the group chat yet?" Brad asked when he stopped by the dealership the following morning to pick up a deposit from Dylan. "The guys all want to know how things went with Robin last night."

So Dylan hadn't exactly been honest with her about the response he'd gotten at Doug's when it slipped out that Robin was helping him on his ranch. A few of the guys were a little more than curious. After all, it wasn't like the woman was making the social rounds in Bronco. Someone speculated that it was because she might think she was too good to hang out with people from the Valley. But so far, nothing about Robin—other than the size of her house and ranch—made Dylan think she was stuck up.

He rubbed the back of his neck, not really knowing how to answer any personal questions if they came up. "Things went great. Mickie turned your list into a spreadsheet for me and downloaded all the photos we took last night and matched them by item number."

Mickie shoved a binder at Brad. "It went from three pages to twenty-six, so I put it all in here to keep things organized."

"Twenty-six pages?" Brad opened the binder, quickly

flipped through the contents then whistled. "You managed to pick out everything on my entire list? In one night? With Robin Abernathy?"

Dylan was already feeling rather accomplished today. Probably because Mickie had also organized the schedule so that he only needed to be in the dealership in the mornings with the other salespeople taking the later shifts. Now he would have the afternoons to work with Robin on the ranch and could dedicate his evenings to sports—both watching and playing. The spirit of competition flowed through him. "Yes. Why? Is that some sort of record?"

Brad gave him a look of disbelief. "It's unheard of. When we redid my bathroom at home, it took Monique an entire week just to decide between two different towel bars. You know that most couples don't normally agree on everything like this."

"Oh, Robin and I aren't a couple," he replied. At Brad's raised eyebrow, Dylan added, "We're just friends."

"You could do a lot worse than Robin Abernathy," Mickie, who'd only moved to town last week, said rather confidently.

"I wasn't aware that you two knew each other," Dylan told his assistant.

"I don't. But Jordan Taylor knows her and he told my sister, Mac."

And this was how rumors spread. While Dylan might be Mickie's employer, her sister had once done his sister a big favor by backing Camilla's restaurant as a silent partner. The overlapping connection between their families was sure to blur some boundaries. But if it meant his office would be this well organized, Dylan was willing to deal with the occasional unsolicited opinion. Especially because the woman was right about Robin.

"Nobody heard anything from me, though," Mickie clarified by making a key locking gesture in front of her mouth. "Because I'm a vault. I don't go around talking about your personal business in front of people."

Brad raised his hand but didn't bother looking up from the binder he was still thumbing through. "I'm a person and you're talking about it in front of me."

Mickie shrugged. "Yeah, but you brought it up first."

Dylan held up his palms. "It doesn't matter who brought it up. Robin Abernathy and I barely know each other."

"I thought you said you were friends," Mickie said, then answered the ringing phone before Dylan could explain. "Good morning. Bronco Motors."

He wasn't quite sure if he and Robin were friends actually. More like associates. Although, he wouldn't mind being her friend. Possibly even something more. Unfortunately, girls like Robin didn't go for guys like him. Dylan had found that out the hard way a long time ago and wasn't going to make that mistake again.

"You working through a play?" Brad asked, apparently done with the list and pictures since he'd closed the binder.

Dylan shook his head. "What do you mean?"

"Your expression. It's the same one you get when you're playing point guard and trying to calculate how to break down the defense."

If only it were that simple. Dylan had no chance of scoring any points with Robin if she found out people were already pairing them up as a couple. Last night when she'd asked if his teammates had said anything about them, Dylan had tried to change the subject. Mr. Abernathy had already acted super weird when he found out his daughter was going somewhere with Dylan. And Robin had responded by getting defensive. Or embarrassed. It was hard to tell yet since he was still getting used to her personality. Suffice it to say, she was visibly flustered by her dad's comments. Just like she seemed to be flustered anytime Dylan tried to flirt with her.

Which was weird because the woman was so confident about everything else.

Brad waved a hand in front of Dylan's face. "Wow, you're really in the zone, man."

"Sorry." Dylan shook his head to clear it. "I guess I have a lot going on in my head right now."

"I bet. So I'm going to go order all of this." Brad held up the binder. "And once I confirm everything's in stock, I'll schedule a demo crew to get started on the house. Do you think the cows are going to be affected by the noise?"

"I don't know," Dylan admitted. "Let me call Robin and ask her."

"Before you do that," Mickie said as she held her hand over the mouthpiece of the phone receiver, "this is the second news station to call this morning asking about the Valentine's Day bake-off. It's that anchorwoman with the big red hair and the even bigger you-know-whats. She said she wants an exclusive interview with, and I quote, 'That sexy car salesman who's running the contest.' She also asked if the winner would get a date with you. What do you want me to tell her?"

Dylan grimaced but hesitated at refusing the free publicity. "Tell her no dates, but I will agree to an interview if it's not live and if she does it here on the lot. Oh, and only if Eloise makes the arrangements."

Up until now, Dylan had refused to make a single commercial for Bronco Motors because he hated the thought of being in the spotlight. But a one-on-one interview for thirty seconds during some late-night news program that nobody watched shouldn't generate too much attention. And since Eloise and her successful marketing firm had taken over the Bronco Motors social media account, he hoped she wouldn't mind dealing with the press, as well. Although, he might need to reciprocate with some babysitting shifts.

Instead of asking Eloise separately, he fired off a quick text in his family group chat because there were so many cooks in this particular kitchen, it helped when they all were going off the same menu. Okay, so maybe that was a bad bake-off analogy. The other benefit to communicating via family chat was that it might save time and give everyone the opportunity to ask about Robin so he'd only have to respond to their nosy questions once.

After he sent that text, he dialed Robin's number.

She answered on the third ring, and he could hear what sounded like a horse neighing in the background.

"Am I interrupting something?" he asked.

"Not really. I'm trying to fit Sparkler with a custom-made magnetic pulse blanket, but her arthritis must be flaring because she's having none of it. What's up?"

"Poor Sparkler. It's tough for an aged athlete to deal with being past her prime. Anyway, Brad wants to know if the noise from the demo crew is going to bother the cattle."

"I'm not going to tell Sparkler that you just called her old. How long is the demo going to take?" Dylan relayed her question to Brad who held up a couple of fingers. "Brad says two days. But I tried to get some of that ugly mushroom print wallpaper off the dining room wall and I'm thinking they'll need at least twelve hours for that alone."

"Yeah, but that won't make much noise. How's the fence looking for the east pasture? I didn't make it that far out when I was there the other day."

"You didn't take the golf cart?" he asked with surprise because that was the first thing he'd tried out when he took over the ranch.

"No, I was embarrassed someone might see me driving it."

"That's not nice," he said, holding back a laugh. "But the east fence is looking the same as the others. Although, it does have that built-in shade structure, which can provide some protection in case the weather gets nasty."

"Okay, so if we can get that fence fixed by this weekend and then get the herd moved over there, Brad's crew could probably start demo next Monday and make all the noise they want."

Now he just needed to find the time—and a crew—to fix the fence. "Does Monday work for you, Brad?"

The contractor gave him a thumbs-up and started typing into his own phone. Mickie was on another call, but Dylan sensed that they were still paying attention to him. He turned his back and lowered his voice. "Are we still on for going to the feedstore this afternoon?"

"Yes," she responded, sounding almost breathless. Then she added, "Why are we whispering?"

Because Dylan was making a big deal out of nothing and acting like they were planning some sort of secret rendezvous. And because he didn't want to contribute to any more gossip about them spending time together. Because gossip led to opinions and opinions led to someone saying that Robin Abernathy was out of his league and he had no chance with someone like her.

Obviously, Dylan knew it. But he wasn't quite yet ready to admit it.

## Chapter Seven

Instead of picking her up at the Bonnie B this time, Dylan met Robin at Bronco Feed and Ranch Supply. One of the things he was starting to like most about her, other than her willingness to share her expertise with him, was that she didn't need to flaunt her family's wealth and success. She didn't drive a flashy car and her clothes were simple, yet fit her perfectly. In the parking lot, Robin walked toward him with the type of confidence that comes from knowing what you're doing and not how good you look. Although, she did look pretty good in those jeans and that fitted wool jacket with her long blond hair blowing loosely around her beautiful face.

How had he only known this gorgeous woman for a few days?

He'd told Brad and Mickie that they weren't a couple

and barely friends. *Associates* was the word he'd stupidly used. The problem was that he now didn't know whether to shake her hand or give her a hug hello.

Apparently, Robin didn't feel the need to waste time with a greeting because she launched right into the purpose of their errand. "I think the stainless steel feeding troughs you have in the barn will last for another few years, but the ones in the outside enclosures I saw have been exposed to the elements for too long and the damage is only going to get worse this winter and spring."

"Right," Dylan said, shoving his hands in his coat pockets. It was supposed to snow again tonight and the temperature was already dropping. But he also wasn't sure what he should be doing with his hands considering the last time he'd entered a store with Robin, he'd been holding hers.

It wasn't like him to be this uncertain around a woman before. Of course, it also wasn't like him to be so uncertain about purchasing so much feed and hay at once, so maybe his uncertainty was stemming more from that.

"Out of curiosity, how have you been getting the cows from pasture to pasture?" Robin's question broke into his thoughts.

"What do you mean?"

"I mean, most ranchers ride alongside the cattle to herd them, but you don't have any horses."

"That should probably be added to your to-do list for me. Both getting a horse and moving the cows to another pasture. Until now, I was doing what Hank said he did, which is to keep the barn doors open so they could come and go from the corral. I knew I'd have to get them out to pasture eventually so that was why I was looking for a good fertilizer to get the grass ready for them to graze. I figured that once I had a spot ready, then I'd figure out how to move them. Probably with the golf cart."

Robin scrunched her face in the most adorable way. Too bad Dylan couldn't enjoy the expression because he knew she was about to deliver an opinion he wasn't going to want to hear.

"Don't hold back now," he told her. "I asked you to help me because I knew you'd be honest and tell me when I was making a mistake."

Just like she had within the first few minutes of him meeting her.

"I'm thinking we shouldn't have picked those custom-ordered cabinets last night. That's money you could be using to buy a trained working horse. You're going to need that more this spring than a re-modeled kitchen."

"Not if you ask my sister Camilla. She said that if I move into that house without a proper kitchen, then she and the rest of the family will set up one of those meal trains where people sign up to bring a casserole on a designated day of the week. They did that to my uncle Stanley after my aunt died and his house was crawling with well-meaning divorcées and widows looking for their next husband. People are already trying to couple me up with any single women they can think of. There are only so many ways that I can politely refuse."

"So it's true what people say about you?" Robin's facial expression was hard to read. "You're relationship averse?"

"I wouldn't say that. I'm just not falling for that whole soulmate thing. You of all people should understand. You're beautiful and a total catch, but you're still single…" Dylan trailed off, realizing he never actually asked her about her relationship status before. His buddies from Doug's hadn't warned him that she was already taken and her father had made it seem like he was eager to see her settled with children, so Dylan had simply assumed—or at least selfishly hoped—that there wasn't someone else. He gulped before he continued. "Right?"

"Uh…" She started to answer but an older woman was exiting the building right that second.

"Look who it is," Mrs. Epson, the woman owned the property neighboring the Broken Road Ranch, said. "What are you doing here, Dylan Sanchez?"

He double-checked the lettering on the sign above the door to make sure they were in fact at the feed-store. Yep. "I'm guessing the same thing you are, Mrs. Epson."

"Buying new wiring for your chicken coop?" she asked, and he realized she was pulling a shopping cart behind her containing two small rolls of metal fencing.

His eyes shot to Robin, silently asking, *Do I even have a chicken coop?*

Robin bit back a smile and said, "The supply of

pellet feed Hank Hardy left Dylan is almost gone and I wanted to show him a couple different brands that might work better for his herd."

Mrs. Epson leaned forward and squinted. "Is that you, Robin Abernathy?"

"Yes, I spoke to you on the phone the other day about Dylan taking over the Broken Road Ranch. Remember?"

"Of course I remember, dear. I just didn't recognize you with your hair down like that."

How did Robin normally wear it? Because this was now the second person from Bronco who hadn't realized it was her.

Robin ran a hand through the loose blond waves and Dylan found himself imagining what her hair would feel like draped across his chest. "Yep, it's me."

"Thank goodness." Mrs. Epson chortled. "For a second there, I thought Dylan had brought some cute little thing to the feedstore on a date."

Dylan didn't like the implication that he couldn't get someone like Robin to go out on a date with him, so he replied by wrapping an arm around her waist and pulling her closer to him. "Who says I didn't?"

Robin made a squeaking sound but didn't pull away. In fact, he felt her body relax against his side, and when Mrs. Epson glanced down to Dylan's hand, he boldly dropped it lower to cup Robin's hip.

"Back in my day, a date usually involved a nice meal." It was hard to tell, but it sounded like Mrs. Epson was making a tsking sound as she maneuvered her cart in front of her. "But you kids do things differently, I guess."

As they watched the older woman depart, Dylan lowered his voice. "Can I ask you a question?"

"I guess?" Robin glanced down at his fingers, which were lightly rubbing along the side seam of her jeans. But Dylan wasn't going to release her when Mrs. Epson might glance back in their direction.

"Do I strike you as the type of guy who wouldn't take you out for a nice meal?"

Robin shrugged, or at least it felt like a shrug the way she was tucked so closely against his side. "It depends on whether you'd describe Bronco Burgers and the taco shop last night as a nice meal."

"Yeah, but that wasn't a real date."

"That's not the impression you just gave to Mrs. Epson."

"I know. Sorry about that, but I didn't like her implying that I couldn't get someone like you to go out with me."

Robin pulled back far enough so that she could stare up at his face. "I'm pretty sure she was implying the exact opposite."

Before he could ask her what she meant, another customer came out of the store and held open the door as though he was waiting for them to enter.

"Thanks, Chuck," Robin told the man as she stepped away from Dylan and headed inside the store.

Dylan had no choice but to nod at the gentleman and follow her.

Knowing he'd need to buy feed eventually, he fig-

ured he'd just order the same stuff Hank already had
stored in the barn. But having found out that the previous owner of his ranch hadn't always made the best
decisions, Dylan had decided to do his own research
ahead of time.

So he was relieved when he saw Robin standing in
front of a pallet of bags that matched one of the better rated brands he'd researched. "This is what we use
for our pregnant and nursing cattle because there's
added nutrients. But this brand behind me is good as
an all-purpose. Do you know if any of your herd are
expecting?"

"Hank said he sold all the bulls two years ago. But
when my brother Felix came out last weekend, he noticed that what I thought was a steer actually still had
all of its equipment. It also has a different color ear
tag, so I'm thinking it snuck in through one of the broken fences. Anyway, one of Felix's professors from
vet school gives students extra credit for pro bono
work and found a few volunteers to come out with my
brother this weekend to examine the rest of the herd."

"That's a good idea," Robin said, again giving
Dylan a sense of relief that he'd made another sound
decision.

Felix had told him that ranches the size of the Bonnie B or the Triple T, which Jordan's family owned,
usually had a veterinarian or at least a vet tech on
staff. Unlike other owners of smaller ranches, Dylan
wasn't experienced enough to know when he needed
a vet and when he didn't. Luckily, he had a brother
who would keep him in check.

"Hey, Dylan, I figured I'd see you in here eventually," Brady Sellers said as he approached them. "How's it going out at the Broken Road Ranch?"

He hadn't greeted Robin, which made Dylan think the owner, like Johnny Lee and Mrs. Epson, hadn't recognized her, either. Instinctively, Dylan reached for Robin and wrapped his arm around her before Brady could act surprised that Robin was with him.

Robin's face whipped around to Dylan's, but again, she didn't pull away. In fact, she fit herself against him just as easily as she'd done outside. Good, because he was starting to become fond of having his hands on her.

"Hi, Brady. You know Robin Abernathy, right?"

Brady's forehead creased in a frown. "Of course I know Robin. I waved at her when she walked in the door before you. I came over as soon as I finished my call."

Robin nodded in confirmation, probably wondering why in the world Dylan had suddenly switched into protective mode. Despite her likely confusion, she remained at his side, though. He didn't hate it.

"So Robin has been helping me out at Broken Road and recommended I buy…" He turned his face toward her. Their noses were inches apart, so he lowered his voice. "How much did you think I should buy?"

"Three pallets of that brand." Robin's voice was raspy, but she pointed at the larger display of all-purpose feed. Then she jutted her thumb at the stacks next to her. "And a dozen bags of the sweet formula."

"You got it," Brady said. "How are you on hay?"

"Hank had a supplier making weekly deliveries," Dylan said. "But I don't love his prices. Especially since I'm hoping to get my pastures back into shape and could be using the extra money there."

Brady and Robin discussed the benefits of alfalfa and sprouts and grass fed pastures and Dylan listened attentively. Then he asked, "So if I go with the hay from Clover's Farm, that's only a few miles down the road from my ranch. I could just buy it from the Clovers directly."

"You could, but Dottie Clover doesn't deliver. Not even locally. I'm one of several distributors she works with who bring their own loaders and trucks to do the transporting and delivery."

"So you're a middleman?" Dylan asked, already knowing the answer.

"You could say that."

"Well, I wouldn't want to cut you out of your share. But at the same time, my supply needs are much smaller and I'm right along the route so it wouldn't be as though your driver would really be going out of the way. Maybe we could come to some sort of agreement."

Brady lifted his chin. "What are you offering?"

Thirty minutes later, Dylan was pushing his receipt into his wallet as he walked out to the parking lot with Robin.

"How did you do that?" she asked him.

"Do what?"

"My family's been ordering from Brady Sellers for the past fifteen years, and never once has he ever given us free delivery."

Dylan shoved his wallet in his back pocket and slipped his arm into place around Robin's waist. "Did you guys ever ask?"

"No, but we shouldn't have to. We give him enough business, he should be offering *us* the discount. Most ranches the size of ours have land dedicated to growing their own. But we still need to supplement with an outside source."

"Can I grow my own?" Dylan suddenly asked. It would actually save him quite a bit of money. "I mean, do my conservation easements allow it?"

"We can look into it. I parked over there. Why are you walking me toward your truck?"

"Because Mrs. Epson wanted me to take you somewhere nice for dinner."

Robin paused. "I don't think that was what she actually said."

"It was what she meant." He maintained a loose grip as he continued walking.

"You know that she's not out here watching us, right? And there's no ice for me to slip on. You don't have to keep your arm around me like this."

"I know, but it's becoming a habit." He released her so he could open the passenger door for her. "Why? Does it bother you?"

Her cheeks were pink and she bit her lower lip as she slowly shook her head.

"Good," he said, then gestured for her to climb inside the cab before he took things further and kissed her right here in the middle of the feedstore parking lot.

\* \* \*

"You never answered my question earlier," Dylan said to Robin after the hostess seated them at the small table for two inside The Library, his sister's restaurant.

"What question?" She'd had a million of them buzzing through her head, but they were all things *she* wanted to ask *him*. Unfortunately, they weren't things she could ask inside the feedstore. Or when he'd been on the phone on the short ride over here answering a question from Mickie when she'd called.

"Whether or not you're single," he said.

"Oh." She didn't know why she felt the need to stall for time, but she wasn't ready to have this conversation. Not here. Not with people pretending like they weren't casting subtle glances their way and wondering to themselves why sexy Dylan Sanchez was at one of the most romantic restaurants in town with plain tomboy Robin Abernathy. Shouldn't he have asked that *before* he'd put his arm around her to pretend they were on a date in front of Mrs. Epson? Robin straightened the perfectly aligned silverware in front of her. "I am not committed to…uh…anyone. Or anything."

Dylan exhaled loudly and nodded. "So, you get it, then."

"Get what?"

"Obviously, you could have your choice of guys, but you're probably like me. You need to be free to do what you want. To not be tied down. Why does everyone think that someone has to be married to be happy? I mean, look at us. We look happy, don't we? Our lives seem perfectly content, don't they?"

She was flattered that he thought she was in high demand when it came to dates. But she was also floored by his suggestion that anyone would possibly compare Robin's lack of a love life to Dylan's reputation as a carefree bachelor.

She didn't want to correct him and admit that men were definitely not beating down her door. But she also wanted to be clear that, unlike him, she wasn't content to remain single.

She twisted the linen napkin in her lap. "I don't know that I'd say I'm opposed to being in a relationship. It just wasn't something I spent much time thinking about when I was younger. I had more important things to work on."

A high school–aged busser brought two ice waters and a basket of chips with queso dip. "Hey, Coach D, did you catch the Bulls game last night?"

Dylan shook his head as he leaned back in his seat. "I only caught the highlights afterward. That dunk right before the buzzer was insane."

The teenage boy's face looked confused. "But they played the Knicks, Coach. You never miss a Bulls-Knicks game."

"I know, Ty, but I had something come up." Dylan shrugged and Robin realized that he hadn't watched the game last night because he'd been with her.

The busser and Dylan exchanged a few opinions about a jump shot and a technical foul in the third quarter before the kid left their table. Robin figured the interruption had distracted Dylan from the topic of her being single, but he picked right back up where they'd left off.

"Yeah, your dad mentioned that you like having projects that take up a lot of your time."

"I did. I do. But I…" She thought of the best way to explain that finding a man was her next project and decided that she couldn't come right out and say that. "Now that my business is off and running, I seem to have more time on my hands."

"For dating?"

If she said yes, would he think she was trying to lay the groundwork for him to potentially ask her out? She didn't want to come across as desperate. Or give off the vibe that she was actively husband hunting. Because that would send him right out the door.

"For socializing." Robin shrugged. "According to my sister, Stacy, I should be going out more in general. In fact, Eloise wanted me to go to the mayor's anniversary party since it was right after she launched the ad campaign for Rein Rejuvenation here in the U.S. But one of my client's horses came down with colic and I was the only one he'd let give him mineral oil."

"I knew I didn't see you there." He pointed his finger at her as though to say *aha*. "I'm actually pretty good with faces."

"Apparently, not everyone in this town is," she murmured, thinking he wouldn't hear over the noise of the other diners around them.

But Dylan heard her and knew exactly what she was referring to. "Yeah, that was weird that Johnny Lee and Mrs. Epson didn't recognize you. I've seen you with your hair both up and down and you look exactly the same to me."

Before Robin could find out if that was a good or bad thing, a server came to take their order.

Dylan didn't even need to look at the menu, which he probably knew by heart. "Let's start with the shrimp spring rolls, the bacon-wrapped brussels sprouts, and the birria torta sliders. Robin, do you want an appetizer?"

"You know that they're meant to be shared, don't you?" Camilla Sanchez Taylor appeared at their table and gave her brother a playful tap on the shoulder.

Robin had been a couple years ahead of Camilla at Bronco High, so they'd never really hung out in the same circles. The Abernathys socialized regularly with the Taylors, but Robin had been too busy working on her latest patent to attend Camilla and Jordan Taylor's wedding. Although, she'd recently gotten to know Camilla a bit more through Jordan's sister, Daphne, who used Robin's products out at the Happy Hearts Animal Sanctuary.

"I was going to share." Dylan rolled his eyes at his sister. "But unlike some people who try to control everything and everyone around them, I wanted to make sure Robin got to choose something, too."

"Are you calling me controlling?" Camilla asked her brother and Robin noticed that they had identical playful smirks.

"I'll take the chicken lettuce wraps," Robin said to the server, who was standing there looking back and forth between her boss and Dylan.

"And a couple of small plates so that we can share because I always share," Dylan told the woman who should retreat to safety before the real fireworks started between the siblings.

Camilla arched a dark brow. "Really? You're not sharing any ideas about how to limit the judges to only five. Both Mrs. Coss, who owns the antiques store, and the mayor said you told them at the anniversary party that they could judge."

Dylan rubbed his temple. "I don't remember it going down like that, but there was a lot going on that night. Kind of like how you have a lot going on with generating enough electricity to run the twelve industrial-sized ovens you want to use for the bake-off. Do you really think we need twelve ovens?"

"That reminds me that Mickie said we don't need as many generators since you have the electric vehicle charging stations. And yes, we need twelve ovens because we finally narrowed it down to twelve contestants."

"I thought I said that we should only allow local residents to be contestants," Dylan said. "I don't mind drawing customers from other towns but, if there are news crews there, I want to make sure we're properly representing Bronco."

"The twelve *are* local residents," Camilla said, then turned to Robin. "By the way, Robin, congratulations on making the final cut."

Robin nearly jumped out of her chair. "But I never turned in any official paperwork."

"Your name was on the sign-up sheet." Camilla

tilted her head as her eyes went back and forth assessing Dylan and Robin. "Although, there might be some complaints about Dylan being a judge if he's openly dating one of the contestants."

"Oh, we're not openly dating," Robin said quickly. A bit too quickly.

Camilla lowered her voice to a near whisper. "Sorry. I didn't realize you guys were keeping it a secret."

"I think what Robin meant was that we're just friends," Dylan told his sister. But he wasn't smiling and there wasn't even a hint of a dimple. Was he mad about the assumption?

"That's not what you told Mrs. Epson. She stopped by here an hour ago to pick up a to-go order and said that you specifically told her that you and Robin were on a date at the feedstore. She was very concerned that you weren't—" Camilla used finger quotes *"—wining and dining your new lady."*

Robin's heart suspended in her chest, bracing for Dylan's explanation that he was only teasing his older neighbor.

"I know she was concerned," Dylan said. "I'm sure she'll be relieved to know that I brought Robin to this fine establishment and didn't just buy her burgers or tacos like I usually do."

Camilla gasped. "Robin, do not lower your expectations for my brother. I know he's been extra busy lately with the ranch, but he can make time for an actual sit-down meal once in a while. Especially on a date."

Instead of correcting his sister, Dylan was looking straight at Robin, his steady gaze practically daring her to deny it. Was this a date? Or was it one of those times she was supposed to know what needed to be done—like the septic plumbing system. All she could do, though, was give him a questioning look.

Finally, he said, "You're probably right, Cam. I won't judge the contest. We don't want to give anyone the notion that I might not be impartial when it comes to Robin."

"Actually, I'm more than happy to withdraw from the contest," Robin said, seizing the opportunity to get out of it before she made a complete fool of herself. "It wouldn't be fair to make him choose between me and this special event that he's been so excited about."

"No." Dylan held up his palms. "We already have the twelve ovens and we wouldn't want our numbers to be off. I insist that I'm more than happy to relinquish all judging duties to whoever else thinks they can do a better job than me."

That's when Robin realized that he was allowing his sister to think they were dating so that he could get out of judging. Although, Robin had just done the exact same thing. Unfortunately, she'd been too late and now she was stuck baking cookies in front of...

"I'm sorry, can we go back to the part where you guys said news crews would be there," Robin said. "As in more than one?"

The server returned just then and asked if they were ready to place the order for the main course.

Something sparkled in Camilla's eyes as she said,

"I'll let you two get back to your date. Teresa, bring them a bottle of the Möet. On the house."

When his sister and the server both left, Dylan's dimples returned. "Why are you looking at me like that?"

Robin lowered her voice. "Everyone is going to see us sharing a bottle of champagne and think we're actually dating."

Dylan shrugged. "Is it so bad if they do?"

"It is if we're only pretending to be dating so that you can get out of judging the bake-off."

"Well, I couldn't very well let you be forced out as a contestant when you're obviously looking forward to it."

When the server returned, she made a big show of popping the cork on the champagne, and anyone in the restaurant who hadn't looked in Dylan and Robin's direction before certainly noticed them now. Teresa filled their glasses and returned the bottle to an ice bucket near their table before telling them she'd be right back with their appetizers.

"Who says I'm looking forward to it?" Robin asked.

"Why else would you have entered the contest?" Dylan tilted his fluted glass toward Robin's and clinked them together.

She couldn't very well admit that she'd only entered it to get closer to Dylan. Especially when her plan seemed to be working. Instead of replying, Robin gulped nearly half the bubbly contents of her glass at once.

"Besides," he said after swallowing his even, measured sip. "That's not why I told Mrs. Epson we were on a date."

A warm sensation spread through Robin's bloodstream, and she didn't think it was the alcohol taking effect this quickly. "Then why did you?"

But before he could answer, one of his buddies stopped by the table to ask about basketball practice and Dylan introduced him to Robin. One of the ranch foremen from the Bonnie B stopped by next and this time it was Robin who made the introductions. But the man seemed more interested in speaking to Dylan.

"My nephew is discharging from the military next week and moving to Bronco before the end of the month. He says he doesn't want his uncle pulling any strings to get him on at the Bonnie B, but if you're looking for someone for the Broken Road Ranch, I could give him your number."

Dylan's brow rose so slightly in her direction, Robin knew she was probably the only one who noticed it. He was asking for her input.

Robin gave a discreet nod. "If Manuel's nephew is anything like him, then I'd jump at the chance to recruit him."

Dylan pulled out his wallet and handed Manuel a business card just as the server returned with several plates of food. By the time they started eating, the moment was lost and Robin didn't know how to redirect him to the subject of why he'd let Mrs. Epson think they were on a date.

In fact, now that she was on her second glass of champagne, Robin was practically convinced that they *were* on a date. He asked her about her company and she explained how she created and patented a line of horse therapeutic products and was toying with the idea of developing a line of skin care products and shampoos for the horses.

He listened intently, leaning his elbows on the table as she spoke and asking follow-up questions. Especially about the ad campaign, which was proving to be just as successful as Eloise had promised.

"My brother Dante certainly lucked out with her and baby Merry." Their dinner plates had already been cleared and the bottle sitting in the melting ice bucket was nearly empty. "In fact, all of my siblings were pretty fortunate in finding their matches."

Robin smiled across the table at him, the champagne giving her the courage to say, "So then what's stopping you from finding yours?"

## Chapter Eight

Dylan was still thinking about Robin's question the next day.

*So then what's stopping you from finding yours?*

He hadn't had a chance to answer it because Robin's brother Billy and his three kids had chosen that exact moment to walk into the restaurant. Charlotte Taylor, Eloise's sister, came inside only a few minutes after them. Billy and Charlotte had dated in high school and had even planned to get married. Dylan wasn't sure of the details, but they'd broken up and Billy had moved away, gotten married and had kids. Charlotte had moved away, as well, but now both were back in Bronco and both were single. Sort of.

Dylan was pretty sure they were back together, but it was none of his business. Just like what was going on with him and Robin was nobody's business.

"So what's going on between you and Robin?" Dante asked late Friday afternoon when they'd finished coaching the kids in Dante's after-school basketball league.

Dylan sighed, sitting down on the hardwood floor to stretch. His body wasn't as young as it used to be, and he was starting to feel as though he was burning the candles at both ends. "Nothing. Why?"

Dante stacked some basketballs on a rack. "Because you told Camilla that you guys were dating."

"No, I said that I told Mrs. Epson that we were dating."

"So are you and Robin dating or not?"

"I'm not sure," Dylan answered honestly.

"Come on. Your reputation around town as a ladies' man is well-earned. You can't seriously tell me that you don't know how dating works."

"Yes, I know how dating works, little brother." He pulled the whistle off his neck and chucked it at Dante. "And I'm not the only Sanchez who had that reputation. Just because you're getting married and became a daddy doesn't mean that you can rewrite the past."

"*Had* that reputation?" Dante asked. "Or *has* that reputation still?"

"Leave it to the teacher to point out the difference in past and present tense."

"Stop stalling and answer my original question. What's going on between you and Robin?"

Dylan lifted his arms. "I don't know. She's been helping me a lot with ranch stuff. I guess you could say we're becoming friends."

"The ol' *just friends* routine, huh? Eloise and I tried to tell ourselves that, too."

"I don't really see a need to define it," Dylan said defensively.

"Eloise and I said that about our relationship, as well. Keep in mind, though, that if you don't define it, someone else eventually will."

Dylan rose to his feet to do some lunges. "Then let them define it."

"I think they already have. Mrs. Epson was in Mom's salon this morning and said she saw you two at the feedstore and you guys couldn't keep your hands off each other."

"So?" Dylan blew out a noisy breath to let his brother know exactly how annoyed he was with their conversation.

"So you never hold me like this when we're shopping." Dante tried to wrap one of his arms around Dylan's waist.

Dylan responded by elbowing his brother in the rib cage. "That's because you're not my friend."

"Why are you getting so defensive?" Dante asked.

"You know why. I don't like having my baby brother all up in my business like this."

"Come on. We've been up in each other's business for over thirty years. Why can't you just be honest about how you feel?"

"Because I don't know how I feel," Dylan said so loudly, it echoed throughout the gymnasium. Several women who were playing pickleball at the nearby court turned in their direction.

Dante waved at the pickleball players but lowered his voice. "Do you *want* to date her?"

"I want to keep hanging out with her. And I want her to keep helping me on the ranch. I like spending time with her, and Mrs. Epson is halfway right. I can't seem to keep my hands off her. But I can't even tell if she has the slightest interest in me. I try to flirt with her, but maybe I've lost my charm."

A pickleball came flying in Dylan's direction and he easily caught it and jogged it back to the court and asked, "Did you ladies lose something?"

He could hear the giggles as he returned to where Dante was standing.

His brother was holding back a grin. "You definitely haven't lost your charm."

"So then I guess the only logical conclusion is that Robin doesn't appreciate my attempts at flirtation."

"Possibly. But Robin is pretty direct and straightforward. When we were in high school, she was super athletic and lettered in several sports. But I don't remember her hanging out at Cubby's after games or going to any dances. She was a straight A student so I always just assumed she was super focused. I work with her sister, Stacy, at the school and I can ask her about it."

Dylan was about to warn his brother not to do that when his phone rang and he saw Robin's name on the screen. His pulse picked up speed.

"It's her, isn't it?" Dante asked. "I haven't seen you blush like that since—"

Dylan pushed the top row of Dante's carefully

stacked basketballs off the cart before walking away to answer the call.

"Hey," he said by way of greeting.

"Are you in a cave?" Robin asked. "There's an echo."

"No, just leaving the gym before my brother chucks a basketball at my head. What's up?"

"Did you ever hear from Manuel's nephew?" she asked.

"Yeah, he called me this morning. He's supposed to fly into Montana next weekend and said he can stop by the ranch sometime. I don't think he has a ton of experience, but at this point, I'll take any reliable help I can get."

"Good," Robin said. "Because I know of a couple of ranch hands here at the Bonnie B who are off duty this weekend and looking to make some extra cash. I told them about your fences."

Dylan looked at his watch. "Do you know what time the lumberyard closes? I better get over there and order some posts. How many do you think I need?"

Robin rattled off a number. "I looked at the property map and did some calculations and while I doubt you'll have to replace every single fence post in the east pasture, it's probably a safe bet to go ahead and order extra since you'll end up using them for the other pastures."

"Any chance you can meet me over there?" he asked, hearing the hopefulness in his own voice.

"Right now?" she asked.

"We can grab dinner afterward," he suggested.

"You have no idea how badly I want to say yes," she said, her throaty voice making him want to groan.

"But I'm in Rust Creek Falls with Eloise and her sister Charlotte meeting with a wedding planner. I haven't tried on a bridesmaid dress before and I've got to tell you, I've never been decked out in so much—or should I say so little—satin in my entire life. I think I'm going to need a jacket."

Great, now he would be thinking about Robin's skin barely covered by a swath of silk. He swallowed the growl building in the back of his throat.

"Are we still set for the livestock auction tomorrow evening, though?" she asked, cutting off his inappropriate thoughts.

"Yes," he said. "I was thinking of making reservations at DJ's Deluxe for afterward."

"I'm not sure you need to do that," Robin said, and he could hear the voices of other women in the background.

Dante had made it seem like Robin could be very direct. And Dylan had definitely witnessed it himself. However, it was only when it involved things that had to do with the ranch. Maybe she wasn't as confident when it came to things like bridesmaid dresses and… whatever this was between them. In which case, he'd give her the opportunity to be as direct as possible.

"Because you don't want it to seem like a date?" he asked, then held his breath as he waited for her response.

"No, I meant because I've never left an auction in under five hours. I doubt we'll get out of there in time to make the reservation. But you can buy me a hot dog from the concession stand and hold my—"

He heard a rustling sound and then a thump. "Sorry, my zipper got stuck and I dropped my phone. We can figure out the details tomorrow. Right now, I have to get out of this dress."

The line disconnected and once again, Dylan was left with the image of her in a state of undress. But more importantly, what had she been about to say before she dropped her phone?

He could hold her *hand*?

He could hold her *beer*?

Did they even sell beer at livestock auctions? It was at the Bronco Convention Center, so they must.

All Dylan knew was that he was going to need to hold *something* tomorrow night.

"So Dante was asking me about you at the school play last night," Stacy said when she came into the kitchen and saw Robin making a test batch of cookies with their niece Jill.

"Why would Eloise's fiancée be asking about me?" Robin couldn't remember where she'd left the pot holder, but Jill was already using it to pull the hot tray out of the oven. She was grateful for the help of her brother's youngest.

"He wasn't asking for himself," Stacy said as she plopped onto one of the counter stools. "He said Dylan was curious to know more about you."

Jill's loud squeal matched the exact same sound of excitement Robin had just made inside her head. "Isn't he the one you've been crushing on, Aunt Robin?"

"Who told you I've been crushing on him?" she asked Jill.

"Seriously? We're making cookies called Heartmelters." Jill held up a faded yellow piece of paper. "Clearly, you're trying to melt someone's heart."

Robin scrunched her nose. "I don't think that's why they're called that."

"You found Great-Aunt Jackie's Heartmelters recipe?" Stacy reached out her hand so their niece could pass the paper to her. "Where was it?"

"In a worn-out tin box on a shelf in the cellar. I was looking for that old-fashioned butter churner and came across it. I figured that it seemed simple enough that I couldn't mess it up. Plus, it's kind of Valentine's themed."

Stacy carefully turned over the sheet of paper. "It says right here, *'When made with the right ingredients and given to the right person, the Heartmelters will have the desired affect.'*" Stacy read it a second time, then added, "I think Aunt Jackie meant to say *effect*, with an *e*."

"So is Dylan Sanchez the right person, Aunt Robin?"

"Right now, I can't even figure out the right ingredients." Robin blew a strand of hair out of her eye with an exasperated sigh. "Or at least the right measurements. It says three handfuls of flour. But whose handful? Aunt Jackie was barely five feet tall. Jill's hands are the closest size to that, but the cookies keep coming out too dense. Same thing happened when I had Mom do the measurements. Stacy, let me see how big your hands are."

Stacy yanked her fist back from Robin's examination to pick up one of the bright heart-shaped cookies from the cooling rack. "Have you tried using your own hand?"

"They're obviously way too big." Robin held up her palm right as her phone timer went off. "I'll have to try another batch tomorrow. Dylan's picking me up in thirty minutes for the livestock auction."

"That sounds like the least romantic date I've ever heard of," Jill said.

Robin took off her apron and Stacy immediately frowned. "You're not wearing that, are you?"

Robin glanced down at the gold-colored sweater that wasn't as low-cut as the last one she'd mistakenly worn with Dylan. "What's wrong with this?"

"It looks like you got it in the same tin box where you found that recipe," Jill said. "Not gonna lie, but the color totally washes you out."

"Are all teenagers this brutally honest?" Robin asked Stacy.

"Let's just say there's a reason why I work with first graders and not middle schoolers." Stacy grabbed a second cookie. "Come on, let's go upstairs and pick a better outfit. I'll tell you what Dylan wanted to know about you."

Jill pumped a fist in the air. "Makeover time. I call dibs on doing Aunt Robin's hair."

Fifteen minutes later, Robin stared at her reflection in the full-length mirror in her sister's room. "Get that makeup case away from me, Jill. I said you guys could do my hair and pick my outfit. And I'm already not loving the outfit. We're going to a livestock auction, not a fancy dance."

The doorbell rang downstairs.

"Can I just do a swipe of mascara and lip gloss?" Jill pleaded.

"I'll do it myself. You go answer the door please, and, Stacy, you go warn Dad that I'm coming downstairs in a dress so that he doesn't make a big deal like he did a few days ago when I borrowed your lipstick."

"Is that why my bathroom looked like a crime scene?" her sister asked.

"Sorry about that. The red was too dark and no matter how many tissues and cotton swabs I used, I couldn't get it to come off."

"That's because it was lip *stain*, not lip*stick*. Uh-oh. I hear Dad talking to him already." Stacy headed to the door. "I'll run down and try to distract him."

Robin took one last look at her reflection. She was wearing a thick knit dress with a floating hemline around her calves. She'd argued that the pale color looked too summery, but Stacy called it winter white and paired it with a tan, fitted leather jacket that perfectly matched her knee-high boots. Jill had used a heated wand to give Robin's hair something called beach waves. As far as makeovers went, it was fairly subtle and she still felt like herself. Just in a dress. Since she didn't have time to change back into her comfortable jeans, all she could do was brace herself for nobody to recognize her.

"Wow," Dylan said as Robin walked into the formal living room where he was standing with her dad, her sister and her niece. "You look amazing."

"Thanks," both Stacy and Jill said at the same time.

"Robin," her father said, hopefully not about to comment on her appearance, "I was just telling Dylan to be sure he looks at the bulls from Greenacres. They have the best breeds and their life cycles tend to be longer than most."

Dylan nodded at her dad's words, but his eyes remained focused on hers, as though he was waiting for her confirmation. Most men would've been over the moon to get some free advice from a successful rancher like Asa Abernathy, taking his opinion all the way to the bank. But Dylan was still looking to Robin for the final say.

Pride blossomed in her chest and she hoped she could live up to Dylan's expectations.

"We'll see who else is in the crowd with an auction paddle," Robin replied. "Because if Birdsey Jones is there, he's going to drive up the bidding on anything he thinks someone else wants. It's like a sport for him."

"Good point." Her father winked at her, then turned to Dylan. "I'd offer you a drink, son, but you're going to need to be stone-cold sober when those auction paddles start flying in the air."

"And you also don't want him drinking because he's driving your daughter, Grandpa," Jill reminded him. Then she told Dylan, "Make sure to have her home by curfew."

"What time is curfew?" Dylan asked politely without so much as a smirk.

"I don't have one." Robin shifted the borrowed clutch higher under her arm—Jill and Stacy had insisted that her normal tote bag she used as a purse wouldn't go with the outfit—and slipped her free hand into the crook of Dylan's elbow. "We should get going."

He said his goodbyes and as they walked toward the door, Robin could hear her niece asking if someone would talk to *her* dad and tell him that she didn't need a curfew, either.

"You cold?" Dylan asked as they made their way down the front porch.

"A little. I wanted to bring a bigger coat but Stacy and Jill were adamant that it would be warm enough inside the convention center. I think they just hate the jacket I usually wear on snowy nights like tonight."

"Or maybe they know how great you look in that dress and didn't want you covering it up."

The girls had said those exact words, but she'd told them Dylan wouldn't even notice. Heat rose along the back of Robin's neck as she realized she didn't mind being proven wrong.

Dylan opened the door for her, which made her extra aware that she was wearing a dress and couldn't just climb inside. He then walked around the cab to the driver's seat and said, "I'll get the seat warmers going."

If she was hoping for the conversation to sound more date-like, as it had the other night when they were having dinner at The Library, she would've been sorely disappointed. As it was, she knew that the entire reason for their outing tonight was business related. They talked about cattle breeds and market prices and his plan to start slow with only one bull while he dedicated his time and budget toward making improvements to his property first. Then she explained expected progeny differences and how he wanted a sire with a positive EPD number.

Dylan found a parking spot toward the front and Robin hurried out of the truck before he could come around and open the door for her again. She would probably be more graceful exiting in the dress than she had been entering it earlier, but she wasn't going to take that chance.

It was snowing lightly, and the cold would have been enough to force her to walk closer to Dylan and absorb some of his heat. But it was the luxury sedan towing a horse trailer that caused Dylan to shoot his arm across the front of her when the driver took the turn too wide.

Before Robin could think better of it, she reflexively curled her hand around his bicep and hugged his upper arm to her side as he pivoted closer to the parked cars and they resumed walking.

"I like that," Dylan said to nobody in particular as he kept his face forward.

Robin glanced back at the sedan and horse trailer that would never find a double-parking spot in this row. "I guess if you didn't have a truck, you could make it work."

"Not that, although I can appreciate their ingenuity installing a tow hitch on a Mercedes." Dylan used his free hand to cover hers. "I like this. When you're the one grabbing on to me."

"Oh," Robin said lamely because she couldn't come up with anything more clever. And also because her heartbeat was vibrating in her eardrums and she couldn't hear herself think.

It only got louder as they entered the arena, which wasn't as deafening as it could be when there was a rodeo going on. They registered and picked up their paddles and Robin tried to concentrate on the animals displayed in the holding area, but it was hard not to notice that there were significantly more men in attendance than women. And she was the only one who was wearing a dress.

Although, maybe that could work in their favor.

## Chapter Nine

"Look how adorable this one is," Robin cooed to the Red Angus bull on the other side of the metal bars. "I just have to have him."

Dylan frowned at Robin's unexpected use of a baby voice and glanced down at the description card attached to the pen. "But this one is from Rosewood Farms and I thought we were looking for a—"

The soft leather of her jacket sleeve did nothing to soften the sharp jab of Robin's elbow into his rib cage.

"But I love this one, Dyl." She searched his face while batting her eyelashes in the most awkward sequence. Was she trying to seduce him or speak in Morse code? It didn't matter because she had looped her arms around his neck and was pressing her chest against his torso as she spoke. "See how his fur has those supercute patches that are the exact same color as my mom's dog Queenie? They would be adorable together."

Dylan might be a greenhorn, but he knew that you never referred to a cow's coat as "fur." Robin was up to something, but he had no idea what. Her thumbs tickled his hairline, causing him to shiver and pull her closer against him.

Robin whispered through her clenched smile, "Is that guy in the blue shirt watching?"

Half the people in this place were wearing blue, or at least denim, so Dylan couldn't be sure. But there was at least one stockier man furtively glancing in their direction.

"I don't know, babe," Dylan said loudly, hoping that he was playing his part. "I don't think we should be buying a bull just because he matches someone's pet."

"Please, Dylan." She lifted on her tiptoes unexpectedly, which caused his hands to slip lower. Her breathless gasp sent waves of desire spiraling through him and he cupped her rounded behind through the fabric of her dress. Her normally sexy voice was even more sultry as she slowly said, "I have to have him. No matter the cost."

He almost responded that he had to have *her*. But he was pretty sure that wasn't supposed to be in this impromptu script. "Uh...how much is it worth to you?"

She leaned forward, her breasts grazing his chest, as she settled her lips against his ear. "Is he still watching?" she whispered.

"Uh-huh," Dylan mumbled, even though he had no idea who *he* was or whether or not anyone was watching. He was too busy trying to control his breathing and not crush her mouth with his.

"Pretend like I'm saying something super arousing to you," she continued, and Dylan almost laughed because he didn't have to pretend anything. "Then, tell me that you'll spend whatever it takes to buy me this bull. Make sure he can hear you."

When she pulled away, she added a coy giggle that must be fake because he'd never heard her laugh like that. She gave him a pointed look and he said his line a little too loudly.

"You're the best boyfriend ever," she said, a little too believably, then lowered her voice. "Now make sure your paddle is in your back pocket and covered by your jacket as you walk away."

Dylan released her long enough to adjust his clothing, which also helped to hide his body's physical response to her.

When she faced away from him, she used her own paddle as a fan, holding it up as she resumed her baby voice and told the bull, "You're going to love living with us. We have a big yard with lots of grass and the sweetest Maltipoo for you to play with. But right now, Daddy promised Mommy some nachos before the bidding starts. The next time you see me, I'll be the one in the stands holding up number 985."

Again, Robin clung to Dylan's arm as she pulled him away, although he noticed that she angled herself slightly behind him, possibly to block the view of his back pocket.

Over his shoulder, he heard her say, "Okay, we

have fifteen minutes before the bidding starts. Come with me."

Instead of getting nachos, though, she led him to where several rows of vendors had set up booths selling everything from sheep shearers to saddles.

"Here." Robin shoved a cowboy hat at him. "Put this on."

"Black's not really my color," he said, sarcastically. "How about the tan one?"

"Fine." She swapped the hats while keeping her eyes glued down the aisle behind him.

"Robin, do you mind telling me what's going on?"

"We don't really have time for that. You need to buy this hat and then make your way to the most northwest corner of the stands. Find a group of other cowboys and sit as closely to them as you can. Better yet, try to blend in with them. Do *not* look for me and definitely do not wait for me. According to the sale catalog, the third bull they bring out should be number 873 from Greenacre Farms."

"I thought we wanted that one from Rosewood with the patches that match your dog Queenie. I'm pretty sure you referred to us as its mommy and daddy."

Robin winced, then shook her head. "Our dog is named Bandit and…never mind all the rest. I'll explain later. Remember, you're bidding for 873, the third bull."

Dylan was more than confused, but so far she hadn't steered him wrong. He was going to have to trust her. "How much should I bid?"

She named the amount he shouldn't go over, then added, "I'll meet you at the sales office afterward."

Robin squeezed into a passing crowd of teenagers in their matching 4-H uniforms and Dylan was left to pay for the cowboy hat. He made his way into the arena area and found a seat in the back row behind several young men wearing the standard cowboy attire of jeans, hats and button-up work shirts.

He'd never felt more like a poser, especially because they were all enjoying plastic cups of draft beer, which Asa Abernathy had warned him not to drink. When one of the cowboys offered Dylan a pinch of Copenhagen, he had no choice but to accept and then pretended to insert it in his lower lip before discreetly slipping the unused chewing tobacco in his front pocket.

Robin had told him not to look for her, but it was rather difficult for him not to notice her. She stood out in this crowd. Not only because she was wearing a dress, which clung to her curves in all the right places, but also because she was…well, she was Robin. And Dylan's eyes now instinctively went in search of her anytime he knew she was nearby.

She was sitting several rows from the front, talking to some people around her and pointing toward the entrance to the arena. The stocky man in the blue shirt who'd possibly been watching them back in the pen area was sitting a few feet away, his eyes carefully trained on Robin. There wasn't necessarily anything creepy about the way the man watched Robin, but that didn't stop Dylan from wanting to punch the guy.

The fast-talking auctioneer called for the first animal and Dylan barely had time to blink before the man yelled, "Sold!"

The second bull took a little longer and several paddles throughout the crowd drove the price higher. By the time the auctioneer finished, Dylan didn't dare look Robin's way again.

He had his sales catalog out and, when he saw the bull in the picture and heard them confirm that it was number 873, a blast of adrenaline consumed him. Leaning back in the seat with his new Copenhagen buddy unwittingly blocking him, Dylan gripped his paddle tighter. This was it. Robin better know what she was doing.

He could barely understand a word the auctioneer was saying, but every time he saw a paddle lowering, Dylan would lift his. When the man yelled, "Sold!" several of the cowboys around him turned to offer their congratulations.

"Thanks, guys," Dylan said. Then asked the one next to him, "By any chance, do you know if the sales office is the same place where I registered?"

The man pointed out directions, and just to be safe, Dylan kept his face averted toward the center of the arena as he passed in front of the crowd on his way toward the exit.

He was paying for his new bull and arranging for delivery to Broken Road Ranch when Robin slipped beside him and gave him a side hug. "We did it!"

"*You* did it," he said, returning the squeeze. Man, he could get used to the feel of this woman. "Although, I'm still not exactly sure what it was you did."

"I got Birdsey Jones to think we were buying the Rosewood bull. Then I sat by him and made him think my boyfriend was in the bathroom so he wouldn't see you buying the bull we really wanted."

That's what Dylan had suspected was happening. But Robin had never struck him as the type to use some elaborate farce to get what she wanted.

"Wait. How long was I supposedly in the bathroom?" Dylan asked.

"You're still there." She tsked at him and gently patted his stomach. "Poor guy. It was the nachos. The doctor warned you about all that cheese, but you couldn't help yourself. It was taking so long that I came to check on you."

"That's not embarrassing at all," he mumbled. When the cashier passed him a receipt, Dylan felt compelled to tell the man, "I'm fine with cheese, just for the record. I can eat it all day long."

"I'm happy for you, buddy," the cashier replied. "I just need you to sign here."

Dylan collected his paperwork as Robin laughed, then grabbed her hand to pull her out of the office.

"I thought you said we would be here for at least five hours," he reminded her as they walked toward the parking lot. "We didn't even have time to get a hot dog."

She smiled. "You can use all that money I just saved you to buy me dinner at LuLu's BBQ."

"I'm glad all that guilt weighing on your conscience hasn't affected your appetite," Dylan told Robin, as she dug into their rib platter for two.

Her stomach dropped. Had he found out that she had no idea how to bake? She scanned the nearby tables to see if anyone had just heard his accusation. LuLu's was usually packed on Saturday nights, but somehow, a table had opened up right when they arrived. Robin was noticing that Dylan knew plenty of people in the restaurant scene. Not only because of his sister's connections, but because he ate out quite a bit. In fact, he actually knew quite a few people from every industry in town, having sold so many of them a car.

When she was convinced nobody was listening, she asked, "What do you mean?"

"You told that Red Angus bull that he would love living with us." Dylan finished a rib and grabbed another.

Robin sagged onto her wooden bench seat with relief, glad he wasn't bringing up everything else causing her guilt.

"He *would* love living with us," Robin insisted. If there was an *us*. "But I don't think he actually heard me."

"I know cows aren't the smartest animals, but that doesn't mean he might not have understood you."

"No, Dylan, I meant that he literally couldn't hear me. That bull had a little marking on his tag indicating a medical condition. According to the sale catalog, which I'd already read in advance, he'd suffered a nonhereditary ear infection that caused long-term damage to his hearing. That's why I went out of my way to talk to him like that. So Birdsey would think I was too naive to consult the catalog."

"That's terrible," Dylan said.

"Terrible that a man would think a woman is naive when it comes to livestock and ranching?" Robin licked a spot of sauce off her thumb. "It actually happens more often than you'd think."

"No, I meant that the bull lost its hearing. Does that mean he won't fetch a good price?"

"Sure he will. He's still pretty valuable as a sire. He comes from good stock and the cause of his infection isn't something that can be passed down. But the Cattlemen's Association requires the disclaimer anyway."

"You could've told me that earlier. Do you know how many times I wanted to turn the truck around and go get him to make good on your promise?"

"You're a softie, Dylan Sanchez."

"Me?" His face was stricken while he looked around as though he thought she might be talking to some else.

"Yes, you." Robin wiped off her hands before picking up a fork to try the coleslaw. "You do know what's going to happen to the calves born on your ranch, right?"

He pointed a rib at her. "As far as I'm concerned, they're going on to a better home on a bigger ranch to live with new friends. That's it. Happily-ever-after."

"Do you mean to tell me that confirmed bachelor Dylan Sanchez actually believes in happily-ever-after?"

"Of course I do. Although, it doesn't always look the same for everyone. My happily is going to be different from your happily. And that's okay." He said the words casually enough, but there was a small trace of defensiveness in his tone.

"Hey there, Robin and Dylan," Phillip Brandt said as he stopped by their table. "Sorry to interrupt, but, Dylan, I need to talk to you about the bake-off and my coconut cream pie. I'm worried that if the weather keeps dropping, my meringue isn't going to hold."

"Camilla said she's watching the weather reports, Mr. Brandt, and is planning to have extra portable heaters if we need them inside the tent."

The man sighed visibly. "That's a relief. But if the weather and the humidity doesn't cooperate, you'll plan to take that into account when it comes time to judge, right?"

Dylan picked up another rib. "Actually, I'm not judging anymore."

"But I heard you love coconut cream pie," Mr. Brandt said. "That's why I'm making it and not my chocolate chip walnut cake. Now I have to rethink my whole strategy. Who's judging?"

"You'll have to check with my sisters. All I know is that I had to recuse myself for—" Dylan gestured across the table at Robin "—obvious reasons."

Robin kicked him underneath the table and he frowned at her.

"Dylan, nobody is going to be worried about you judging in favor of your girlfriend." Mr. Brandt lowered his voice. "No offense, Robin, but I tried the cinnamon rolls you brought to the bake sale at school, and they aren't winning any contests."

Robin would have been insulted if the man's assessment had been completely accurate. "Those weren't *my* cinnamon rolls. My sister made them and when people brought them back for a refund, she blamed it on me."

"Why would Stacy do that?" Dylan's expression didn't appear shocked, though. He looked like he was trying not to laugh. "Not that my brothers wouldn't have probably done the same thing to me."

"Because I'm a horrible—" Robin stopped before she could say the word *cook*. It was bad enough that Phillip Brandt was confirming her lack of culinary skills. "I'm horrible at cinnamon rolls. Or anything else that requires yeast and rising and being patient. Anyway, I'm not even making those for the contest, Mr. Brandt. I'm making something else. And it's going to take first place."

Okay, maybe that was laying it on a little thick, but Robin couldn't very well back down from a challenge. Especially when she knew the risk Mr. Brandt would be taking with that meringue if there was wet weather.

"Nobody stands a chance against my lemon tart," Mrs. Sellers, the feedstore owner's wife, said from two tables over. "Dylan, you might as well give me those free oil changes now."

And that was how the Valentine's Day Bake-off Trash Talking Tournament started. Solar, the purple-haired teenage barista from Bronco Java and Juice, came over to make a case for her German chocolate brownies, and Gary, the middle school PE teacher, said that any insult to the cheesecake he was making in honor of his late aunt Hildy was an insult to Aunt Hildy herself. May she rest in peace.

Dylan slouched lower in his seat as everyone argued over his and Robin's head. "Maybe I shouldn't have made this a locals-only contest."

Robin wanted to laugh at his obvious discomfort. "If this is how they argue with their neighbors and friends, imagine what would happen if you had a bunch of out-of-towners show up."

"Fair enough," he said before slathering a hunk of corn bread with LuLu's famous honey butter.

Robin reached across the table to help herself to one of his French fries. She was midbite when someone asked, "Robin, what are you making for the bake-off?"

"Hopefully her cinnamon rolls," Mrs. Sellers said under her breath and Robin shot the woman a dirty look.

She opened her mouth to respond, but someone else complained, "Dylan, you can't judge a contest that your girlfriend's in. That wouldn't be fair."

"He's recused himself from judging," Mr. Brandt explained before Dylan could correct the crowd and announce that Robin wasn't his girlfriend. Several heads nodded as though that fixed everything.

She braced herself for public humiliation when Dylan held up his palms. "Mr. Brandt is correct, I won't be judging. If you have any questions about the bake-off, I'd encourage you to stop by Bronco Motors and speak with my office manager, Mickie. She's also posted all the contest rules on our website. Now, if anyone sees LuLu or our server, will you please tell them that we'd like some banana pudding to go and the check. I have to get Robin home before she misses curfew."

"Well, that was one way to make an exit," Robin said fifteen minutes later when Dylan was driving her to the Bonnie B.

"I know. I wasn't expecting LuLu to be out of banana pudding."

"That's not what I meant, Dylan."

"I know that, too." He glanced at her across the dimly lit interior of the truck and her muscles tensed. "But when I find myself in awkward situations like that, I tend to make light of the situation and use humor as a distraction."

She knew she shouldn't ask, but she couldn't stop herself. "What was awkward about the situation?"

"You have to ask?" he said.

"I mean, I know which part was awkward for *me*," Robin clarified. "But which part was awkward for you?"

"I don't do crowds very well," Dylan finally admitted and Robin had to do a double take. "I'm better in a one-on-one situation, or in smaller groups."

"You were homecoming king at Bronco High and played college basketball, with several games nationally televised. I've seen you in stores and in groups of people and you don't exactly come across as an introvert."

"Okay, being homecoming king was out of my control. When they announced it at the football game during halftime, I didn't even take off my helmet to be crowned. And when I played college basketball, I was part of the team and didn't draw any more attention than anyone else. I refused to do media interviews because I don't like anything that could potentially cause a scene. What happened inside LuLu's wasn't exactly a scene, but it felt like I needed to make some sort of big announcement and I'm not the type who enjoys making big announcements. I'll leave the speeches to Mayor Rafferty Smith, thank you very much."

Robin studied his profile as he drove. "What sort of big announcement did you think you'd be making inside a barbecue restaurant?"

"You heard them. It was like they were looking for confirmation of some sort, and I didn't exactly know what to say."

Robin pursed her lips, doubting that he was going to say it aloud. But she also didn't want to let him off the hook. "You mean about whether or not I'm your girlfriend?"

"That's part of it," he said, causing her lungs to stop working for a second. "But I've been so on edge about this entire bake-off. I recently hired a couple of new salespeople so that I could spend more time at the ranch. I pay them a salary, but they also work on commission and get factory bonuses for every car they sell. If I want to keep spending time on the ranch, I need to keep my employees happy. And my employees are happy when they're making sales. So as much as I want to increase business, I don't want to be the focal point.

I also don't want to do or say anything that's going to scare you away."

Robin shifted in her seat toward him. "You're not going to scare me away, Dylan."

"That's because you've never been to a Sunday dinner with my family."

"Is that an invite?" she challenged.

"I wouldn't do that to you just yet," he said with a chuckle. But what Robin heard was *It's still too soon.* And it was. Maybe she shouldn't be pushing for more.

Reluctantly, she changed the subject. "So we've got three guys lined up tomorrow to come work on the fencing at the Broken Road."

"You're coming with them, right?" Dylan asked as he turned onto the county highway leading to her ranch. "Not to do the actual fence work, but maybe just for an hour or so to help me lay them out. I'll bring breakfast burritos."

Damn him, and his knowledge of food being the way to her heart.

"I can come out for one hour," she said, knowing full well that she'd be giving up valuable time in the kitchen. "When is Felix coming with the interns from the veterinary school?"

"Nine. So you might be gone by the time they get there."

"I really shouldn't miss that, though," she said, already going back on her limit of one hour. "And I guess I should take a second look at your stables and see if I need to do anything before I bring a couple of horses over for Monday when you need to move the herd to that east pasture."

"Robin, you don't need to give me any horses. You've already done so much for me."

He was right about the last part, but not the first. "I'm not giving them to you. I'm only loaning them to you until you can get your own. Also, if I'm going to be the one helping you herd them, I'd prefer a horse I'm comfortable riding rather than that old golf cart Hank Hardy left behind."

Dylan reached across the center console, found her hand in the dark and squeezed it. "I can't even begin to tell you how much I appreciate all your help. I promise that one of these days, I'm going to make it up to you."

Her fingers interlaced with his, but instead of enjoying the comfort of his hand, she wanted to bang her forehead in frustration. If she were trying to play hard to get, she certainly would've lost the game by now. This was why she was a horrible negotiator and paid full price for tractor tires and hay delivery.

She'd gone from just sending over cowboys to probably a full day's work without even giving him time to counteroffer. Could she make herself sound any more available? Or any more eager to be with him?

She should be focusing her energy on figuring out how to make her recipe work, not running out to see Dylan every time he offered her a flash of his dimples and a hot meal. It wasn't as though she had unlimited amounts of open days in her calendar. Her choices were to either spend time with him, or to spend her time baking so that she wouldn't end up a laughingstock when she came in dead last.

It was too bad she couldn't do both.

## Chapter Ten

The second smartest thing Dylan had ever done was hire Mickie to run his dealership office and free him up to spend more time on the ranch. The smartest thing he ever did was ask Robin for her advice that day he met her.

As promised, she arrived with three employees from the Bonnie B early the following morning. Dylan had a stack of breakfast burritos and a load of lumber and barbed wire ready and waiting for them. One of the benefits to being a car salesman was access to used cars on the lot and Dylan was able to borrow a trade-in truck to help haul supplies out to the east pasture. After showing the men the property map and reviewing the number of posts they'd need, Robin caught a ride back to the barn with Dylan just in time to meet Felix and the two volunteer vets.

"Nice to see you again, Robin." Dylan's brother reached out to shake her hand. Felix normally saw mostly domestic pets at his practice, but one couldn't live in a ranching town without having some experience treating larger animals. "How's Bandit doing?"

"Better since the treatment," Robin said, smiling. "And the bland diet."

"I have to take a second load of equipment out to the crew," Dylan told her. "Do you guys need anything from me?"

"We've got it covered," Felix said. "Go build your walls."

"Fences," Dylan corrected his brother. "I'm mending fences."

"Oh, that's right. I guess I'm just used to you building emotional walls."

"Robin, don't listen to anything he says about me. He's just jealous that I set a better pick than he does."

"We'll see about that at the next family basketball game," Felix said. "I've been practicing my jump shot and Shari says my calves look better than ever."

"Shari is just being kind because she can't say anything good about your dribbling." Dylan was reluctant to leave Robin, but he was also looking forward to some good physical labor. It was cold, but he needed to sweat. And pound something that wasn't his brother's head.

He spent the rest of the morning pulling out broken fence posts and hammering new ones into place. When they ran out of barbed wire, he and the workers returned to the barn together for lunch and to re-stock their supplies.

Dylan wasn't surprised to see his dad's car in the driveway, nor was he surprised to find his father in the stables with Robin.

"Hey, Dad, I see you met Robin."

"I didn't need to meet her, son. Robin and I go way back. Her family's ranch is on my mail route." Aaron Sanchez claimed he had more insight into anyone in town based purely on the contents of their mailboxes. "Anyway, Robin was telling me how she was going to bring a couple of her horses over and I was telling her about that time you rode a tame, old mare on the beach in Baja and ended up going for an unexpected swim."

"She wasn't that old," Dylan muttered, making Robin choke back a laugh. "And she definitely wasn't tame."

"All I'm saying, Robin, is if you get my son on a horse, make sure you bring a few ice packs and an Ace bandage."

"You've got it, Mr. Sanchez."

His dad held up a palm. "No, please call me Aaron."

"You know I can't do that, Mr. Sanchez," Robin replied. "My mom and dad would be mortified."

"What your dad should be mortified about is his golf swing," Dylan's father said, then explained, "Asa and I go to the same driving range."

Robin's smile was warm. "I'll be sure to mention it to him the next time we have dinner."

"Speaking of family dinners," his dad said, and Dylan closed his eyes, knowing what was about to come next. "Did Dylan tell you about our family dinners every Sunday?"

"As a matter of fact, he *has* mentioned them," Robin said.

Both Robin and his dad were now staring at him expectantly. But there was no way Dylan was going to invite Robin to his parents' house for a Sunday dinner. He'd only invited one other woman and that had been a mistake he'd never repeat.

"I forgot to tell you and Mom," Dylan said, "but I'm not going to make dinner tonight. I've got too much going on with the fence repair and getting the house ready to start demo tomorrow."

"Well, good luck giving your mom that excuse," his father said. Being absent from Sunday dinner usually required advance notice or a doctor's note. "I'm refereeing a game at the rec center at two and need to get there early to remind the pickleball club to take down their net."

If Robin was disappointed by the lack of invite, her face didn't show it. In fact, after saying goodbye to Dylan's dad, she said, "The stables actually look to be in pretty decent shape, probably because they haven't been subjected to any wear and tear the past twenty years."

"I'm surprised Hank didn't park his golf cart in there," Dylan said.

"Judging by the tire tracks in the old straw, I'm pretty sure he did."

Dylan didn't know whether to laugh or roll his eyes, so he did both. "I'm going to need to sweep out all that muck and lay some fresh straw before you bring the horses."

"I already took care of it."

"When?" Dylan asked.

"While you were out riding the range, cowboy." Robin nodded at his hat. "I see you're making good use of your souvenir from the livestock auction."

He adjusted the felt brim, knowing he was already getting it dirty with his dusty hands. "I should've gone with the black one. Hey, are you staying for lunch? I ordered a tray of sub sandwiches from Bronco Brick Oven Pizza."

"Yeah, the delivery guy just left before your dad got here. I put the rest of them in the kitchen fridge, which is going to need to be moved out to the barn once demo starts."

Dylan was actually thinking the stables would be a better place to move the fridge... "Wait, what do you mean you put *the rest of them* in there?"

Robin wiped the back of her hand across her lower lip, as though she could hide the evidence. "Well, your dad was hungry. And since I only had one breakfast burrito this morning, we sort of helped ourselves."

"You didn't even wait for me?" Not that Dylan blamed her.

"It's after one. I kept thinking you guys were going to break for lunch and show up any minute but I got hungry."

"I should probably take whatever is left to everyone else who is patiently waiting."

"I did patiently wait." Robin playfully shoved his bicep.

Dylan clamped his hand over hers, locking it into place as he spun her around and backed her into his arms. "You waited for maybe ten minutes."

She shrieked with laughter and tried to wiggle away, although it didn't feel as though she were putting that much effort into it. In fact, she seemed to be pushing her backside directly into his—

"There you are, Dylan," Felix said as he came around the corner. His brother's eyes widened briefly before his face broke out in a wide grin. "I didn't mean to interrupt your little wrestling match, but we're about wrapped up here. I was going to see if Dad and Robin left any lunch for us."

Robin gasped, causing her chest to expand directly above Dylan's forearm since he was still hugging her from behind. "We only had one sandwich each, Felix Sanchez. There's at least ten foot-long subs left. Were you planning to eat more than ten?"

Chuckling at the way she'd effortlessly responded to his brother's teasing, Dylan added, "Not if he wants to fit into his wedding tux."

Felix's eyebrows rose at the hint of a challenge. "I bet you twenty bucks I look better in a wedding tux than you, Dyl."

"I'd take that bet, except you know full well you're never going to get me in one of those."

"Yeah, I forgot. You're the Last Sanchez Standing." Felix used his fingers to make air quotes. "Remind me what the prize is for winning that title? Eternal loneliness and regret?"

"I'll go grab the sandwiches from the fridge while you boys argue about tuxes and other manly pursuits." Robin's voice was less playful as she easily stepped out of his embrace. Dylan felt a cool breeze at the empty place where she'd been. "And then I need to take off to get the horses ready."

Dylan watched her walk away, and then he shoved his brother. "Why do you always try to embarrass me like that?"

Felix shrugged. "It's what big brothers do. Don't act like you weren't plenty embarrassing when Shari and I were first dating."

"First of all, I doubt I was. Second of all, Robin and I aren't exactly dating."

"Really? Because that's not what it looked like when I walked around the corner a few minutes ago and caught you guys all cuddled up and giggling."

"I don't giggle. Also, I haven't exactly asked her out on a date. I might be working my way up to that, but I'm certainly not ready to invite her over to our parents' house for dinner."

"I get it." Felix nodded.

Apparently, though, Felix did *not* in fact get it because as the sun began to set, he was in the lead car as several family members pulled into the driveway of the Broken Road Ranch.

Scratch that. It wasn't several members of his family. It was his entire family.

"Dad said you had too much work to do here tonight

and couldn't make it to Sunday dinner at our house. So we brought Sunday dinner to you." His mother was carrying a foil-covered casserole dish as she scanned the barn and stable area until her eyes landed on the Bonnie B truck and horse trailer. "Oh, is Robin still here?"

Robin heard several voices coming from outside as she closed Buttermilk's stall door. She thought the demo team wasn't starting until tomorrow morning, but it sounded like a crew of construction workers were shouting orders in the yard.

When she exited the stable, she nearly froze then took a few steps back.

It was the entire Sanchez family. The men were moving several wooden benches in front of a make-shift firepit that Robin could've sworn hadn't been there a couple of hours ago. The women were setting up a table with trays of food and plastic cutlery. Earlier, she'd stood there awkwardly when Mr. Sanchez had brought up Sunday dinner, shifting her feet as she waited to see if Dylan was going to take the bait and actually invite her.

He hadn't.

Then his brother had made that comment about Dylan wanting to stay single and she'd beaten a hasty retreat. Now she was shifting on her feet wondering if she should try to slip into her truck and drive away before anyone noticed her.

Too late.

"Robin," Eloise called across the yard, baby Merry

wrapped securely against her chest. "Do you know if there are any napkins or paper towels in the house?"

Was Robin supposed to answer this question? Were they trying to see how "at home" she was on the Broken Road Ranch? Luckily, Dylan answered for her. Or them.

"Actually, I put a lot of that stuff into bins and hauled it out to the stables because they're tearing the roof off tomorrow and starting construction. If we would've known you guys were all going to show up, then maybe we could've had it all set up for you."

She wondered if he even realized he was using the term *we*, as in he and Robin. Clearly Sofia and Camilla had caught it because they were looking at each other with raised brows and smirks. But since Dylan seemed to have not known his family was coming, it wasn't like he'd invited her to eat with them.

She wiped her hands on the back of her jeans. She wasn't as dirty as she had been earlier when his dad and Felix had been talking to her; she'd changed when she'd gone home to get the horses. But still, the other women in Dylan's family looked so stylish.

As everyone worked together to light the bonfire and set up the food, she got Dylan's attention and jerked her chin toward the parking area. He shook his head no. Frowning at his refusal to come talk to her, she flicked her wrist to subtly wave him over.

He looked around and when nobody appeared to be watching him, he slowly made his way over to where she was standing and whispered, "You can't leave."

"I can't stay, either," she said through gritted teeth. "It's a family dinner."

"If you don't stay, they'll track you down eventually and drag you to my parents' house some other time. It's best to just let them get it out of their system and then everyone can move on."

She wanted to ask him what they'd be moving on from, but the sound of a horn stopped her.

Stanley Sanchez pulled up with Winona Cobbs in the passenger seat. It took a couple of minutes for the older couple to exit the car.

"Sorry we're late," Uncle Stanley said. "I couldn't take the driveway as fast as I wanted to because I'm not driving my 4x4."

Everything suddenly got very quiet and everyone's eyes turned to Dylan. "Sorry, Uncle Stanley, but I had to sell it. That sedan is just as nice, though. It's safe and reliable and the Gravity Defying Green is an exclusive, hard-to-get color."

"You sold your uncle's truck?" Robin whispered beside him.

Dylan lowered his voice to match hers. "No. It was a truck I'd let him borrow from the dealership anytime he wanted to impress his girlfriend and take her off-roading in the mud. Apparently, my family members, as well as Stanley's doctor, thought it might be a little too dangerous. Not necessarily for my uncle, but for the other drivers who often had to move out of his way."

Robin nearly snorted. Okay, now that was adorable. Totally reckless, but also a bit touching. Clearly

Dylan cared about his relatives and tried to help them out when he could.

Denise Sanchez, Dylan's mom, slapped her hands together. "Food's ready. Robin, since you're the guest of honor, you go first."

Initially, she was supposed to know where the paper towels were kept, yet now she was the guest of—

She squeaked when Dylan gave her a light tap on the behind. "Hurry, before it gets cold."

"Why don't you-all start." Robin held up her palms. "I need to go wash up first."

"Don't use the kitchen sink," Sofia warned. "That faucet smells super funky."

Robin smiled. "I learned that lesson the first time I was here."

As she walked toward the temporary wash station she'd set up next to the hose bib protruding from the side of the barn, she could hear Dylan explaining to his family about the septic system.

When she returned, she was relieved to see that people were already piling their plates with food. She didn't want to be the cause of everyone missing out on a hot meal. Of course, that ship had most likely already sailed. It was February in Montana. Absent a freak heat wave, the temperature was going to make everything outdoors feel pretty frosty. Although, by the time she filled her plate with a thick slice of lasagna, salad and garlic bread and then sat on one of the benches in front of the warm flames, she felt as though she could've been at a beach bonfire during July.

The Sanchez family made her feel right at home, even though she had to remind herself several times not to get too comfortable. Everyone took turns teasing each other and no one was immune from being on the receiving end of a family joke, including the in-laws.

During a story about the previous Tuesday when Dante took his third-grade class on a field trip to the library where Shari worked, Dylan leaned closer to Robin and whispered, "You doing okay?"

She nodded. But when he continued to study her, she asked, "Why wouldn't I be?"

"Because my family can be a lot."

"Dylan, I have siblings, too. Plus, something you don't have yet."

He nodded his chin toward his relatives sitting around the fire. "What do you have that could possibly be any worse than this?"

"Two teenage nephews and a teenage niece. If you think having your brothers tease you about your eyebrows is bad, try having a thirteen-year-old girl list all the reasons why your closet needs a complete makeover. Just wait until baby Merry gets older. Teenagers do wonders for the self-esteem."

"From where I'm sitting, and I have a very good view…" Dylan paused and allowed his eyes to travel up and down the length of her body, causing Robin to shiver. But not from the cold. "I don't see a need for you to change a thing. Although, if she was the one who picked out the dress you wore yesterday, then I can't say that I object to the results."

Robin gulped, hoping that everyone would assume her cheeks were flushed because of the fire. "I'll be sure to pass along your approval."

"Please do that. As a youth basketball coach and the occasional substitute referee when my dad can't make it, I'm all too familiar with that generation's ability to trash-talk. If possible, I'd prefer to be on your niece's good side in advance."

In advance of what? Was he planning on meeting the rest of her family anytime soon?

"Then Dante comes out of the bathroom holding the very wet copy of *Diary of a Wimpy Kid* he just rescued from the toilet and runs straight into Mr. Brandt," Shari said, and everyone laughed. "Thank goodness the man owns a dry-cleaning business."

Robin realized she'd missed the last half of the story because she'd been whispering with Dylan.

"Speaking of Phil Brandt," Denise Sanchez said. "Mallory was in the salon the other day and told me that the bake-off can't come soon enough. She said that if she has to try one more bite of her husband's meringue from the outdoor test kitchen he set up in their backyard, she's going to learn how to change the oil in his car herself."

"She might as well learn anyway," Uncle Stanley said. "Because there's no way Phil is winning the free car service for a year. My Winona and her chocolate torte are going to take first place."

"Miss Winona," Sofia said, "if you don't mind my asking, what are you going to do with the prize if you win the bake-off? You don't have a car, do you?"

"I'm entering the contest to win the gift certificate for dinner at The Library. And for bragging rights. I'm sure everyone has their own reasons for entering, right, Robin?"

The psychic smiled at her knowingly and Robin wanted to slink lower on the bench until she could completely disappear from sight. *Please don't say it out loud*, Robin tried to convey to Winona in the hopes that the psychic could read minds.

"I didn't know you entered the bake-off, Robin," Mr. Sanchez said before taking another bite of food. "Is that why you can't be a judge, Dylan?"

"Of course it's why," Uncle Stanley said. "The man can't very well judge a contest when both his girlfriend and his aunt are contestants. People might think he's biased."

Winona's bracelets jingled as she patted Stanley's hand. "I'm not Dylan's aunt."

Stanley's weathered face looked stricken by the correction. He immediately said, "*Yet.* You mean you aren't his aunt *yet.*"

Winona seemed to have not heard her fiancé's attempt to confirm the status of their relationship and continued, "But I do agree that people probably won't think it's fair if Dylan votes for his girlfriend's cookies."

Robin's brows shot up in surprise. "How did you know I was making cookies?"

Everyone turned toward her, their facial expressions clearly suggesting that it was fruitless to even question Winona Cobbs or how she knew things. The woman just did. In reality, the real question Robin should have asked was, *Why do you think I'm Dylan's girlfriend?* But at this point, everyone in town was erroneously assuming that Robin and Dylan were a couple. Especially because neither one of them was doing anything to correct people.

"What kind of cookies are you making, Robin?" Camilla asked.

"I'm just glad to know it's not your cinnamon rolls," Dante said at the same time.

"First of all, the cinnamon rolls weren't mine, Dante. You've worked at the school with my sister long enough to know that Stacy always gets assigned paper plates and utensils when there's a potluck. Second of all, Camilla, I'm making a family recipe I found in my great-aunt's old recipe tin."

"Can't go wrong with a recipe called Heartmelters." Winona nodded and Robin stared at her in amazement. How did the woman sense these things? "It's probably how your great-aunt got your great-uncle. The trick is in the measurements."

Robin exhaled loudly. "You can say that again."

"If you need some help working the recipe and trying different techniques, I'd be happy to help," Camilla offered.

Sofia scrunched her nose. "Mmm, I might not do that if I were you."

"Why not?" Dylan asked. "Robin is going to need all the help she can get."

A chorus of *uh-oh*'s and *oh no*'s came from Jordan, Boone, Felix and Uncle Stanley. Dante laughed out loud at his brother's blunder and Mr. Sanchez dropped his head in his hands. Even baby Merry stirred from her nap and began to fuss.

"I didn't mean it like that, you guys." Dylan glowered at his male relatives. Then he softened his expression when he faced Robin and said, "I promise I didn't mean it like that. I meant I wanted Camilla to help you so that you do well in the contest."

"You're not making it any better, bro." Dante was still chuckling.

Robin crossed her arms. "You don't think I can do well on my own?"

Obviously, she couldn't, but she didn't want Dylan to know that. Yet.

He set down his plate and put his arm over her shoulders. "I think you are great at everything you do. Why else would I want your expertise out here on Broken Road Ranch?"

"Sof, why don't you think it would be a good idea for Camilla to help Robin?" Boone asked his wife. Dylan looked as though he wanted to hug his brother-in-law for getting the conversation back on track.

"Even though Camilla isn't a judge, she's providing one of the prizes and she's helping with the organizing." Sofia stood and started collecting plates for the trash. "It's probably best if we avoid all appearances of favoritism."

Robin wanted to point out that, despite her bragging to Mr. Brandt, she wasn't expecting to win anything. In fact, she wanted to withdraw from the contest entirely. But it was too late to quit without causing more gossip. At least she'd already succeeded in making Dylan notice her, which was the reason she'd signed up in the first place.

"I'm sure Robin will do just fine in the bake-off," Mrs. Sanchez said as she stood to help with the cleanup. "Winona will, too."

"Wait." Mr. Sanchez rose, followed by everyone else in the family. "We can still sample the desserts, even if we're not judging the contest, right?"

"I should hope so," Dante said, patting his stomach before reaching to take Merry from Eloise. "If I have to help set up all those balloon arches and party tents, I should at least be rewarded with my choice of baked goods."

The family continued to joke and tease each other as they made quick work of putting out the flames and packing up the food. The goodbyes were short since the heat from the fire was gone and the cold had settled in. It was rather chaotic as everyone was heading to their cars, especially since Uncle Stanley nearly sideswiped the back bumper of Jordan's SUV as he executed a too-wide U-turn.

Robin thought she'd be able to slip away quickly, but her truck with the empty horse trailer was parked near the stables and the other vehicles were blocking her in.

"So I'll see you tomorrow morning to get the cattle out to the east pasture?" Dylan asked as he caught up to her near the driver's side door.

"Bright and early," Robin replied.

So far, any time they'd ended one of their days

or outings together, they hadn't so much as hugged goodbye. But she couldn't stop staring at his mouth, wondering what it would feel like to have his lips on hers, even for a brief moment.

He must have read her mind because he took a step toward her. Just when she thought that he was going to lean down and kiss her, Robin panicked and flung her arms around his neck, averting her face to the side as she went in for the hug.

"Okay, have a good night," she said, giving his back two solid pats. She might as well have been a teammate telling him "good game."

She pulled back from the awkward embrace quickly and hopped into the cab of her truck, needing to get out of there before she embarrassed herself any further.

As she drove away, she peeked in the sideview mirror and saw him standing in the middle of the driveway, his hands tucked in his coat pockets as he watched her taillights.

Yep. She was already a goner.

## Chapter Eleven

"Why couldn't I have used the golf cart, again?" Dylan called out over the sound of mooing.

"Because you wanted to be a real cowboy," Robin yelled back as she easily trotted along in the saddle, keeping her side of the herd in a straight line.

Yeah. Except that was before he realized that riding a horse wasn't any easier as a thirty-four-year-old man than it had been as a fourteen-year-old. It was impossible to grow up in Bronco and not have ridden at least once. Several of Dylan's high school friends had ranches and he'd gone riding with them a handful of times. But when you're competitive and you like to be the best at something, it was easier for him to find other activities he excelled at. Like playing basketball and driving fast cars.

Robin must've seen the grimace on his face as he

awkwardly shifted in the saddle because she shouted, "Just trust Buttermilk and do what I do."

The pale horse Robin had brought for him had seemed old and slow at first, but as soon as she had caught sight of the cattle, the mare proved that she knew exactly what to do and was in her element. As much as Dylan wanted to remain in control of the reins, as soon as he relaxed his grip, he realized that he pretty much just needed to hang on and let Buttermilk do her thing.

Besides, his ranch wasn't huge. It wasn't like they were going that far. In fact, within fifteen minutes, they had the herd inside the new fencing of the east pasture and Robin hopped off her horse to shut the gate. Which was probably for the best since Dylan's thighs were already burning. He always thought of himself as being in pretty good shape, but this morning he was using muscles not normally needed on the basketball court.

Robin, on the other hand, had made riding look entirely effortless and fluid. She moved with her horse as though they were one and, unlike him, did not bounce around in the saddle. Dylan could only wish that someday he might have a third of her ability. In the meantime, all he could do was hope that she didn't think less of him for his lack of skill.

Whenever he didn't know how to do something, he found that if he at least acted confident, most people would be none the wiser. So as they turned to head back toward the stables, Dylan asked, "How come I ended up on the horse named Buttermilk and you got the horse named Maze Runner?"

"I think we both know the answer to that," Robin replied with a teasing grin.

So much for his theory of fake it until you make it. "Was it that obvious?"

She reined her horse closer to his. "If it makes you feel better, I've seen worse. One time, my brother Theo brought someone he was dating out to the ranch and she wanted to barrel race. Theo wrongly assumed that since she asked, she had at least some experience, so he put her on one of our fastest mounts. Let's just say there was lots of screaming, plenty of tears and no more dates after that."

"So what you're saying is that I should be proud of the fact that I'm not crying?"

"Well, you haven't cried *yet*," Robin said before making a clicking sound, encouraging her horse to pick up the pace. His mare took that as a sign to follow suit and suddenly Dylan was holding on for dear life.

He would've told Buttermilk to stop succumbing to peer pressure, but he had to keep his jaw firmly clenched so that his teeth wouldn't rattle. Thankfully, the return trip to the stables was much quicker since they didn't have the cows with them this time.

When he was finally able to heave himself out of the saddle, Robin was already walking Maze Runner around the yard, allowing her to cool down.

"At first, I was worried about having to come back for you, Dylan. But you definitely showed signs of improvement. In fact, those last few minutes I completely stopped worrying that you were going to fall and mess up your pretty little face."

"You're lucky I can't let go of Buttermilk's reins as I walk her," Dylan said with a hint of challenge.

Robin's blond ponytail whipped around as she tossed her head back and dared, "Or else what?"

Last night, Dylan got the impression that she'd wanted to kiss him goodbye but had chickened out at the last minute. He'd settled for the hug, not wanting to push her for something she wasn't ready for. But judging by that pretty-face comment and the way the corner of her full lips tilted into a smirk, she was practically begging for it.

"Or else I might find something better for your mouth to do than tease me."

She bit her lower lip as she boldly studied him. "Do you really need both of your hands free to do that?"

Groaning, Dylan took a step toward her to prove that he didn't need any hands at all, but before he could lower his head to hers, they were interrupted by the engine of a loud truck.

They both turned toward the driveway to see Brad arriving with his work crew. For a second, Dylan had completely forgotten that the whole reason they were on the horses this morning in the first place was to move the herd for demo day.

Robin's fingers grazed against his hand as she reached for the reins. "Here, I'll tend to the horses while you go meet with Brad. They need to be watered and rubbed down before I load them onto the trailer."

Warmth spread along his skin at the spot where she'd touched him and, instead of releasing the reins, he used his other hand to clasp her waist. "You're not leaving yet, are you?"

She lifted her face toward him, her voice low and husky as she asked, "Do you need me to stay?"

"I *want* you to stay," he clarified.

"I can stay for a few minutes, but I really need to get the horses out of here before all the construction noise gets going."

"Then you'll come back?" he asked.

She looked at a spot past his shoulder. "For lunch?"

A truck door slammed nearby and Dylan knew that he had only a few more seconds to have her this close.

"And for this," he said before brushing his mouth softly against hers.

It was the barest of kisses and only a promise of what he had planned for the next time he got her alone. Yet, the sound of her indrawn breath would stay with him the rest of the morning.

Robin's lips were still tingling from where Dylan had kissed her a few hours ago. At least, she was pretty sure it had counted as a kiss. If she had blinked, she would've missed it. That was how quickly it had taken place. By the time she returned from taking the horses back to the Bonnie B, the delivery driver from Bronco Brick Oven Pizza was pulling in behind her.

Since they needed to replace the roof and porch before the next snowfall, the crew was working at a swift pace and took their lunch breaks in shifts. This meant that people were in constant motion on the property, and she didn't get another moment alone with Dylan.

Robin was talking to the service techs from the county and showing them the best spot to install the water line for the house when the younger tech asked her if she was single. Before she could answer, the man's face turned a bright shade of red and his eyes darted to something behind her.

Not something. Some*one*.

Dylan walked up with a clenched grin that didn't quite meet his eyes. Something was wrong. He put his arm around Robin's shoulders as he spoke. "Babe, I need to get back to the dealership and see about a fender bender that happened during a test-drive." He must not have noticed her blinking in confusion over the term of endearment because he kept talking. "Brad has a question about the color scheme we want in the master bedroom so when you get finished here, would you mind going over that with him?"

"Uh, sure," she said, even though they hadn't selected any color scheme, certainly not for something as intimate as his master bedroom. But maybe that was what Brad had wanted to ask her about.

"I hope you're lucky enough to find a woman like this one day," Dylan said to the still-blushing service tech. Then he dipped his head and kissed Robin directly on the mouth. This time, it wasn't simply a brush of the lips. It was searing and hot and almost made Robin forget they had an audience watching them.

Dylan pulled back slowly, his eyes seeming to search hers while his voice confidently said, "Thanks, babe."

Robin was in a complete daze as she stared at Dylan

striding away. The last time he'd called her babe was when they'd been putting on an act for Birdsey Jones at the livestock auction. Had his kiss just been another act? Because it had certainly felt real to her.

The older water tech, the one who seemed to be in charge, cleared his throat. "Ma'am, I think we're all good here if you want to let the others know that we'll be running our backhoe on this side of the property for the next hour or so."

"Right," Robin said then walked on wobbly legs toward the house where Brad was supervising a tractor loading rotted roof shingles into a dump truck. Yelling over the noise, she relayed the information about the backhoe then asked, "Did you want to talk to me about a color scheme or something for the master bedroom?"

"Not yet," Brad said as he made a hand motion to the tractor driver, who shut off the engine. Resuming a normal tone, he added, "I told Dylan that we would worry about paint colors later."

"Oh." Robin reached up to touch her lips then realized it would be a dead giveaway so she rubbed the creased line on her forehead instead. "I wonder why he told me to come talk to you about it now."

Brad guffawed. "Probably because he noticed the way that young fella over there was looking at you."

Robin jerked her head up. "What do you mean?"

"That kid from the county water authority was having a tough time taking his eyes off you and, judging by the expression on Dylan's face when he stomped over there, he probably wanted the boy to know that you were already spoken for."

Spoken for? "You make it sound like Dylan was being territorial."

As soon as Robin said the words, all the pieces clicked together. Calling her babe. Referencing their color scheme for the *master bedroom*. Kissing her so boldly like that while everyone was watching.

Brad must've been able to tell that she'd been slow to pick up on all the signs because he chuckled again. "Growing up on a ranch around a bunch of men, Robin, you've surely had a pair of young bucks fighting over you a time or two."

If she had, she'd been completely oblivious to it. Just like she had been a few moments ago. She wanted to ask Brad if he thought that meant Dylan liked her. But even she knew how naive the question would sound. This wasn't high school when your best friend would ask you to talk to their crush for them.

"Uh-huh," she managed to mumble, then changed the subject to the condition of the roof shingles. "Can any of these be salvaged?"

"Maybe enough to build a little chicken coop later on. But that's going to be way down on the list of things to get done around here." Brad spoke a bit more about the fascia boards and the porch railings, but Robin had difficulty focusing on his words.

She was still thinking about Dylan's kiss and his intent behind it. She wanted him to kiss her because he couldn't not kiss her. Not because he was trying to make someone believe they were a couple. Next time his lips burned against hers, if there ever was a next time, Robin hoped they wouldn't be standing in the middle of a construction zone with at least ten other people buzzing around them.

"We're good here, if you need to take off," Brad said, bringing Robin back to the present moment. Had he noticed that she wasn't paying attention? Probably. But he was likely just as eager to get back to work.

"If you're sure you don't need me, I do have a few errands I need to run." Such as picking up more baking powder at the grocery store because she wanted to practice a few more batches of cookies before the bake-off in two days.

Brad pulled out his phone. "Just leave me your number in case something comes up."

Robin didn't mind the man having her contact information, but surely he should be reaching out to Dylan first. After all, it was his property. But since he might be busy at work, it wouldn't be a bad idea for Brad to have someone to call as a backup.

Robin wasn't gone from the ranch longer than two hours when she received her first text from Brad. Although, technically, it was a group text including Dylan so Robin didn't really need to answer. She set the phone down on the kitchen counter and put on her apron only to hear another notification alert.

It was Dylan's response to Brad.

I think the septic people are coming tomorrow, but you'll have to ask Robin if that will interfere with the county water guys.

And that's how it went for the next couple of hours. Every so often, Brad would have a question and then Dylan would ask her what she thought. But at no point did he text her directly without Brad acting as a chaperone of sorts. He definitely didn't call her to explain why he'd referred to her as babe out of the blue and then publicly kissed her.

Finally, after several more failed attempts at cookies and another episode of the reality dating show she was hooked on, Robin was about to turn out her bedroom light and call it a night when her phone pinged again. It was from Dylan and the first thing she noticed was that Brad was not on the text.

Thank you again for all your help today. I'm still at the dealership dealing with the insurance paperwork.

She typed back a response. Did anyone get hurt in the accident?

Just the sidewalk sign in front of Mrs. Coss's antiques shop. She wasn't happy, understandably.

Robin wanted to ask him about what happened earlier, but maybe he'd already forgotten it. It was Dylan Sanchez, after all. He'd probably kissed plenty of women the same way he'd kissed her.

While she was still deciding what to type, another message appeared on the screen.

I'm not going to make it out to the ranch tomorrow. I'll be knee-deep in bake-off preparations and trying to find a place to hide that ridiculous pink shirt Sofia thinks I should wear for the news interview.

So Robin wouldn't see him at all before the contest. Maybe that was a good thing.

Or maybe it would give her too much time to think.

In that case, try to get some rest. Have a good night. Robin pushed the send button, determined to put the man completely out of her mind.

Except that only left her thinking about the bake-off and how she was going to make a complete fool of herself.

Dylan looked up to the sky to send a prayer of thanks that this was the warmest, sunniest Valentine's Day on record in Bronco. They didn't need the heat lamps or the removable walls of the huge party tent, which meant the spectators who came to watch could easily slip off into the lot to look at the cars.

Which was the main reason he was hosting the event at Bronco Motors.

"Your mom and sisters certainly outdid themselves," his dad said as he patted Dylan's back.

"I know," he admitted, even though he'd never really doubted their abilities. Sure, the balloon arches and heart garlands strung across the lot were a tad too much. But having the red and white cars parked in a row facing the street was a brilliant touch. As was the media campaign that Eloise had managed.

"That was quite the news interview you did yesterday," his dad continued. "Did Mom forward you the video clip?"

"Yep." Dylan nodded. So did half of his teammates, Mickie and Mrs. Epson, his new neighbor. But he hadn't watched any of the videos on his phone. In fact, he was keeping his eye out for any sign of the white news van and the redheaded anchor who'd slipped him her number, which he'd passed straight to Mickie since Dylan had no need of it.

Eloise had done a rehearsal of sorts with Dylan beforehand, going through possible interview questions so he wouldn't stumble or mess up during the recording. But when the anchor asked him on camera if any of the contestants would have a chance at winning a date with him, his mind had immediately flashed to Robin. Yet he'd managed to respond, *Well, one of our contestants has been happily married for forty years and I think his wife would rather him win the free oil changes.*

"You ready for this?" Camilla asked as she came over holding a tiny device that was supposed to clip to his shirt.

He took a step back. "Don't you think a wearable microphone is a bit overboard?"

"The DJ said it'll look more natural than having you walk around with a cordless mic in your hand." Camilla batted his hand away as she tried to clip the small wire to him.

"You're pulling on my chest hair!" Dylan's accusation blasted through the speaker system because apparently the microphone was already switched on.

"Then stop pulling away," Camilla said, her voice also serenading the, thankfully, still-empty lot.

Sofia ran over to take the small battery box attached to the wire and turned it off. "Fess up, Dylan, and tell me where you hid the pink shirt. Mickie said she saw it hanging in your office yesterday, but you expect me to believe it's suddenly vanished?"

"It's not like I could wear it anyway, Sof." Dylan grabbed the microphone from Camilla's hand and clipped it to his not pink shirt. "See, I'm already miked up."

The DJ put on the first song, a predictable love ballad, to test the speakers. Dylan grumbled. "Please tell me we're not going to be playing stuff like this the whole time. This song is going to make people want to slow dance, not buy cars."

"Eloise came up with the playlist," his brother Dante said as he joined them. He'd taken the day off work to help and was pushing baby Merry in her stroller. "She said it will inspire romance."

"I need it to inspire sales," Dylan replied.

Both of his sisters groaned in unison. Camilla said, "It's a wonder you get any female customers at all. You have no idea what a woman wants."

Dylan was inclined to agree, but Sofia took it a step further. "He has no idea what *he* wants, either."

His jaw dropped, then he quickly recovered. "What's that supposed to mean?"

Camilla put her hands on her hips. "It means why haven't you asked Robin out yet?"

"I took her out to your restaurant, Cam. Remember? You made a big deal about it and sent a bottle of champagne to our table."

"What?" Dante turned to their sister. "You never sent me and Eloise a bottle of champagne when we were first dating."

"That's because Eloise was pregnant. And you were eating enough free dessert that I figured the bottle of champagne would be cheaper this time. Stop distracting Dylan, so he can answer my question. Why haven't you asked Robin out on a proper date that doesn't include buying something for your ranch first?"

Dylan lifted his arms in exasperation. "Because I don't know that she wants to."

"There is no way our brother can be this clueless," Sofia said to no one in particular.

"Trust me, he is," Mickie said as she approached with a spray of red roses.

"I thought I was paying you to be loyal," Dylan muttered under his breath.

"No, you're paying me to keep you organized," his office manager with excellent hearing said. "Besides, honesty is a form of loyalty. And if I'm being honest, part of your problem, Dylan, is that you've never had to work for it."

Dante laughed, but Dylan was scratching his head. "What are you talking about? I'm a hard worker."

"With your business and your ranch, sure you are. But from what I've seen, you've never had to work too hard when it comes to women." Mickie stage-whispered to his sisters. "You'd be amazed how many young gals come in here wanting a so-called test-drive with your brother."

Camilla made a gagging sound and Sofia slammed her palms over her ears. "Don't want to hear it."

"She means test-drive the cars!" Dylan used his two fists to make a steering wheel motion, but his thumb caught on the wire twisted around his lapel.

"Do I?" Mickie asked rhetorically. "All I'm saying is that when you have ladies doing the asking all the time, you never really learn how to do it yourself. Anyway, I have to get these flowers to the judges' table."

"I know how to ask women out," Dylan insisted, hearing his words echo in the speakers.

"You really need to stop fidgeting with that microphone," Dante told him before pushing the stroller toward the arriving contestants and guests.

## Chapter Twelve

Robin tilted her head as she squinted at the commercial-grade oven, trying to figure out how to even turn the thing on. This was nothing like her oven at home.

"You turn this knob in the middle to preheat it." The pretty woman at the cooking station next to Robin's pointed at the row of high-tech controls. Gabrielle Hammond. Each contestant had their names custom embroidered across the matching red aprons Camilla had provided.

She'd seen Gabrielle in the grocery store the other day and the checkout clerk, who knew everyone in town, mentioned that the woman was Bronco's newest resident. Then the clerk alluded to some sort of mysterious background that Robin hadn't asked about.

"Thanks," she told Gabrielle with a smile. She could only imagine what it was like moving to a new town and having everyone asking questions that were none of their business.

"I don't think I can work on this stove," Mr. Brandt, who was on the other side of Robin, said to nobody in particular. "The burner is bigger than the one I have at home. Does medium heat mean regular stove medium heat? Or does this stove put out more heat because it's so much bigger?"

Gabrielle left her station to show him the temperature settings. "If you're in doubt, I believe they provided a cooking thermometer, too. You can use mine if you need it."

Thank goodness Robin wasn't making anything in a saucepan or skillet or she'd have to forfeit right now. She tried to concentrate on her recipe, but she hadn't realized she would need to triple the recipe to make enough for the judges and the spectators. Okay, so that meant three cups of butter. Did she have that much? She should. If not, she'd have to borrow some.

The contest rules had been posted online, but she'd forgotten to read them until this morning when Mickie had sent a last-minute email asking for Robin's signature on some paperwork. One of the rules was that each "kitchen" needed to be set up exactly the same. Everyone had brought their own ingredients, but they were required to use the provided measuring tools. Which meant that Robin couldn't use the antique punch ladle she'd used at home when she'd gotten the best results. It was supposed to be three—make that nine—ladles of flour. She looked down at her cupped hands and tried to gauge the amount in handfuls. She'd never done a practice batch using her own hands for measurement. Was it too risky to try now? Probably. But she had no choice.

There were four rows, with three kitchen stations in each row. There wasn't a ton of space between the rows, which meant the contestants could easily talk to each other if they wanted.

"Now Shep is the one keeping me up at night," she heard Deborah Dalton, the contestant at the station behind Mr. Brandt, say to someone in her row.

"Why would you be worried about Shep?" Bethany McCreery asked. The wedding singer was directly behind Gabrielle with her niece, Molly McCreery, right between them at the station behind Robin. Normally, Robin might find it odd that a ten-year-old could successfully compete in a cooking contest where she was the only person using a step stool to reach the counter. But Molly's mother had died six years ago, and the girl had become like a surrogate mom to her two younger siblings. So she was probably used to helping out in the kitchen at home.

"Because he's almost thirty and shows no sign of finding a significant other," Deborah Dalton responded to Bethany.

"Thirty's not that old," Mr. Brandt said over his shoulder.

"Thirty is ancient," Solar, the purple-haired barista, called out from her row behind Mrs. Dalton.

"Don't fuss at the boy, Deborah," Winona Cobb said from her station in front of Robin. "Shep will settle down."

"Do you know when, Winona?" Mrs. Dalton asked, a hint of desperation in her voice.

But the psychic seemed to be too focused on the contents of her saucepan because she absently replied, "He'll find love when it's his turn."

"My dad already had his turn," Molly said very matter-of-factly.

Robin's heart would've broken for the little girl and Jake McCreery, her widowed father, if Winona hadn't looked up from her pot of chocolate long enough to turn around and thoughtfully say to the girl, "Some people get two turns."

"I know I got two turns," Dylan's uncle Stanley said as he sidled up next to Winona.

"Stanley," Winona scolded her fiancé. "You're not supposed to be over here talking to the contestants."

"I know, but I wanted to come over real quick and tell you that I spoke with Camilla and she said we could have our reception at The Library. I know how much you love the food there."

"I can't talk about that when I'm focused on my ganache," Winona replied. Robin should be focused on her own baking, but she kept getting distracted by everybody else around her. And the heavenly smells.

"You want to have our reception at The Library, though, right?" Stanley asked again, not quite willing to give up. His insistence kind of reminded Robin of another Sanchez man she knew.

"What I want is to make this chocolate torte." Winona used her fingers to sprinkle another pinch of sugar to her pot.

Robin realized this was now the second time she'd heard Winona seem reluctant to give Stanley a definitive answer about their wedding date. Robin, whose brother Billy had once been left at the altar, hoped there wasn't something else going on between the older couple.

"Excuse me, Mr. Sanchez." Robin waved the man over. "Do you know if the rules say anything about us getting access to more ingredients if we run out?"

"I can go check," Stanley offered. When he left, Robin congratulated herself on being able to distract him with an errand.

"Do you need something, Robin?" Gabrielle asked. "I brought way more than I'll need."

Before Robin could answer, Deborah Dalton called out, "Gabrielle, you're new in town, right?"

The woman smiled politely at Mrs. Dalton. "I am."

Oh boy. Robin knew exactly where this was going. Mrs. Dalton was going to try to set up Shep with the first single woman she could find.

"If you have some extra butter," Robin said to Gabrielle before the conversation could become uncomfortable, "I think I'm going to need another cup."

"Is unsalted okay?" Gabrielle asked, but was already walking toward the huge stainless steel refrigerator at the back of the tent.

Wow. Robin was getting pretty good at the whole distraction thing. She'd just successfully diverted two awkward moments. Of course, she hadn't even cracked a single egg yet, or figured out her flour measuring technique. But it wasn't like there was a time limit or anything.

"Ninety minutes, ladies and gentlemen," the DJ announced in between songs. "We have ninety minutes remaining."

Robin's heart sank as she realized she'd missed that information in the contest rules she'd only briefly glanced over this morning. Trying to refocus, she mentally calculated how long it would take to bake nine dozen cookies.

"Here you go." Gabrielle passed her a package of butter right as Dylan made his way into the tent, followed by a news camera.

Robin had seen him thirty minutes—she glanced at the large digital clock she hadn't noticed earlier on the stage—make that thirty-three minutes ago when he'd given a very brief welcome before turning things over to Mayor Smith who was the master of ceremonies. She remembered Dylan saying that he wasn't looking forward to being the center of attention today, but he seemed to be holding his own as he stopped by each station and asked the contestants what they were making. It wasn't until he was talking to Solar, the barista, that Robin realized he wasn't looking in the direction of the camera at all. In fact, he seemed to stay one step ahead of it at all times, as though he was purposely blocking out the fact that he was being recorded.

"I need to go check something," Gabrielle murmured and slipped away from her station right before it was her turn for an interview. Which meant Dylan had to go straight to Robin.

"Robin Abernathy," he said, flashing those irresistible dimples that made her stomach do somersaults. His eyes seemed to fill with relief as he focused on her face. But maybe that was just her imagination. "Tell us what you've got going on here."

Since all she had in front of her was an empty mixing bowl, she held up the package in her hands. "I have this butter."

He glanced down at the package. "Yep, that's butter all right. What do you plan to do with it?"

"I'm making cookies," she said her voice sounding high and squeaky.

"I'm making cookies, too," Molly McCreery said behind her. "Double fudge peanut butter chip cookies."

The cameraperson pivoted toward the child, bypassing Mr. Brandt and causing the boom mic to hit his bald head.

As far as baking contestants went, apparently, there was more news interest in a ten-year-old girl than in a sixty-year-old man.

"Sorry, Mr. Brandt," Dylan murmured as he stepped around the man and followed the camera to the next row. "I guess we'll be coming back to you."

Dylan moved into place behind Robin. They were now back-to-back and if she wanted to reach behind her, she could probably touch him. But she needed to get something in her mixing bowl.

"Miss Molly here is our youngest contestant," Dylan said. "Tell us about the contest so far, Molly."

"Well, Mrs. Dalton is looking for a girlfriend for her son and Ms. Winona said people find love when it's their turn and my daddy might get two turns. Except it's not my turn yet, because I'm only ten and I like making cookies more than I like boys."

"Me, too," Molly's aunt Bethany said, and Robin had to bite back a giggle. She knew that Bethany was likely making it clear to Mrs. Dalton that she wasn't a candidate for still-single Shep.

"I'm making a coconut cream pie with a meringue topping in case anyone's interested," Mr. Brandt said, still waiting for his turn in front of the camera.

"We know, Phil," Gary, the only other man in the contest, called from the back row. Gary, like everyone else in town, had heard his fair share of angst about the meringue and the weather.

The camera moved to Mr. Brandt, who talked at length about his meringue techniques, and Robin heard Dylan whispering to Mrs. Dalton, "They're coming to your station next, and I feel it's only fair to warn you that Shep is going to kill me if I let his mom tell everyone who watches the news that he's single and available."

"He's the only one of my sons not settled down yet and he's almost thirty." She wiped her hands on her apron. "Why you boys do this to us poor mamas is beyond me."

Robin turned on her electric hand mixer so she wouldn't have to listen to Dylan's response. She creamed the butter, wondering what Mrs. Dalton must think of a woman Robin's age still not married, especially since she was older than Shep. And the only man she'd even thought about settling down with was, right this second, probably explaining why he planned to stay single indefinitely.

She switched off the mixer and bent down to grab the sack of sugar from the shelf below right as Dylan was moving out of the way of the camera. When he bumped into her, she dropped the bag.

"Here, let me get that for you," he said, squatting directly beside her to pick up the sugar. Their legs were touching as they both stood at the same time. He reached in front of her to place the container on the counter, letting his arm brush slowly past hers as he retreated.

Robin shivered, but didn't dare look at his face since she had no doubt he'd do something else to make her blush.

"Is anyone else hot under this tent?" Mr. Brandt asked and, for a second, Robin thought he'd witnessed what had just happened between her and Dylan. But then she saw his saucepan boiling over.

The man let out a string of curse words that made Molly and Solar giggle. "Great, now I need to start over with my coconut filling."

Robin glanced at the clock and realized she needed to get moving.

According to the recipe, she was supposed to cream one handful of sugar into the butter. Which meant for this batch, it would need to be three. She looked at the measuring cup with uncertainty. She didn't have enough butter or enough time to do this a second time. Her fingers were tingling and before she knew it, Robin was pouring the sugar directly into her palm.

Robin finally got into a rhythm with her cookies and was using her heart-shaped cutter on the rolled out dough when the DJ announced, "Thirty minutes left."

"You'll see when you have kids one day, Bethany." Deborah Dalton must have already finished because she was back to chatting with everyone around her. "What about you, Gabrielle? Do you want kids?"

Alarm bells went off in Robin's head, because she, too, had been asked that personal question before.

Gabrielle, who had plated her dessert and appeared to be tidying up her station, didn't bother to look at Mrs. Dalton when she replied, "Actually, I already have a daughter."

"Oh," Mrs. Dalton said, disappointment in her tone. "I hadn't realized you were spoken for."

"I'm not." Gabrielle took off her apron and set it on the counter. "Good luck, everyone."

As the woman walked away, Solar turned around holding her tray of German chocolate brownies. "I don't think she loved your questions, Mrs. D."

"Oh no." Mrs. Dalton's face fell. "Do you think I got a little too personal?"

"Maybe a little." Robin took the first pan of cookies out of the oven and slid in her second. The woman's heart was in the right place, but not everyone, especially newcomers to Bronco, wanted to discuss their business in such a public setting.

"You're right. I better find her and apologize." Mrs. Dalton hurried after Gabrielle.

Soon, only Robin, Winona, Molly and Bethany were left at the cooking stations. Robin was fanning a pot holder over her last batch of cookies, trying to cool them down quicker.

"Those look lovely," Winona said as she hefted the enormous cake platter holding her chocolate torte. "You followed your great-aunt's recipe to a T. I hope you're prepared."

"Prepared to be humiliated when I come in last," Robin muttered under her breath.

But the older psychic must've heard her because she replied, "Oh, you're going to win. And lose. And then win again."

Robin gaped at the woman as she walked away under the weight of her chocolate torte. What did that even mean?

Dylan was relieved that this event was about to come to an end soon. It was a good thing he hadn't judged the contest because he, Mickie and the other salespeople had been bombarded with test-drives and sales paperwork. Even his dad and brother Dante, who used to help out in the office on the weekends, had to be called in for reinforcements.

Earlier, he'd been happy to turn over the master of ceremonies duty to Rafferty Smith, who'd thankfully taken over the interviewing, as well. Robin was the last one to get her cookies to the judging table, and even though Dylan had tried to downplay the whole romantic Valentine's Day backdrop, he thought it was pretty cool that she'd matched the theme with her red, heart-shaped cookies.

But now that the judges were conferring behind the

table, Dylan knew he was going to be needed soon for the big announcement. Rodeo sweethearts Jack Burris and Audrey Hawkins were comparing notes with Sadie Chamberlin Grainger, who owned the Holiday House gift shop. Dylan expected Kendra Humphrey to be the toughest judge since she owned Kendra's Cupcakes and baked professionally. But DJ Traub, the owner of DJ's Deluxe restaurant in Bronco Heights, seemed to be having a tough time making up his mind.

While they were waiting for Mayor Smith to tabulate the scores, Dylan slipped one of Robin's cookies off the tray and took a nibble. His eyes nearly rolled into the back of his head as he moaned in ecstasy. His second bite was bigger and practically melted in his mouth. This had to be the best thing he'd ever eaten. Who knew Robin was just as good in the kitchen as she was on the ranch?

His eyes scanned the crowd looking for her and spotted her laughing at something her sister was saying. Man, Robin was beautiful. Dylan's family was right. He needed to ask her out. There was no way he could let a woman like her slip past him. He reached for a second cookie and was halfway finished with it when Mayor Smith waved a paper in front of him and said, "We have a winner."

The DJ announced that the results of the contest were in, and the crowd made their way under the enormous tent. Dylan was pleased to see how much more standing room there was outside the tent because so many of the cars on display had already been sold and moved off the lot.

Dylan had ditched the wireless mic a while ago when he'd accidentally asked an older customer if he was buying the convertible for his daughter and it turned out the man was actually there with his much, much younger girlfriend. Whoops.

Taking the handheld mic from the DJ, he said, "Ladies and gentlemen, thank you again for coming out to Bronco Motors and spending your Valentine's Day with us. I'm not as good with the big speeches as our mayor is, so I'll keep this short and sweet. Third place in our bake-off contest goes to Gary Peterson for his Aunt Hildy's Cheesecake."

There was a round of applause as the PE teacher came up on the stage to shake Dylan's hand and claim his prize.

Dylan looked down on his sheet and had to swallow a brief lump of disappointment before he could continue. "Second place goes to Robin Abernathy for her Heartmelters. And I will say that if you get a chance to try one, they're pretty incredible, folks."

More applause and Robin came on stage. Instead of shaking her hand, like he did with Gary, Dylan pulled her in for a tight hug. He inhaled the scent of vanilla lingering in her hair and the mayor tapped him on the back. "That's enough, son. She can't claim her gift certificate with you holding on to her like that."

Dylan, unsure of what had just come over him, quickly released her and cleared his throat. "And the winner of the first annual Bronco Motors Bake-Off and the recipient of a dinner for two at The Library, as well as a year's worth of free car service, is Gabrielle Hammond for her Love Is All Around cake roll."

He scanned the audience for Gabrielle, who he hadn't met yet. Mickie had assured him that the woman was new in town and qualified as a local. But she hadn't been at her station when Dylan had done the interviews with the news camera. Finally, he spotted a brunette making her way toward the stage before pausing to look to her right. She must've seen something or someone she wasn't expecting because instead of coming on stage, she made a beeline to her left and disappeared into the crowd.

That was weird.

When the applause died down, Dylan covered for the winner's absence and said, "We'll keep Gabrielle's trophy and prize in a safe place so that she can claim it later. Thank you everyone for coming out to Bronco Motors and Happy Valentine's Day!"

He turned over the microphone and grabbed another one of Robin's cookies as a reward for getting through that announcement. Then he swore to himself that he was going to stay away from public speaking events for the rest of his life.

The crowd slowly trickled away as the DJ concluded with the song from *Dirty Dancing* about having the time of one's life. If Dylan was being honest, the music playlist had been pretty good and kept people entertained while the baking was going on. Mickie was already directing the tent people and restaurant equipment suppliers to disassemble everything and get the lot back to normal. Contestants were passing out samples of their baked items and Dylan swooped in to take a plateful of Robin's cookies before everyone else descended on them.

Several people stopped him on his way to his office and he smiled and chatted briefly but didn't offer them a single cookie. When he set the plate down on his desk, he thought about locking the door to keep them safe inside. Then realized that he was being absolutely ridiculous. It wasn't like he couldn't ask Robin to make him another batch.

Where was Robin anyway? He needed to see her and make sure she wasn't disappointed at her second place finish. Maybe he could console her if she was. The thought of pulling her into his arms again had him striding out of his office only to find her carrying an arrangement of roses to the reception desk.

She looked up and saw him, her pretty face tilted as she gave him a suspicious look. "What are you doing hiding in here?"

He waved her over to him and when she got close enough, he grabbed her hand and pulled her inside his private office. "It's not that I'm hiding myself, so much as I'm hiding those."

He pointed to the plate of red hearts on his desk and Robin laughed, the musical sound making his chest feel lighter. He sat on the edge of the desk and held one of her hands as she stood before him.

"What did you put in these things?" He used his free hand to offer one to Robin. "They're amazing."

"Thanks." She took a bite and her face softened as

she chewed lightly. "Wow. They actually came out better than I expected."

Desire coiled through him like a spring and he couldn't take his eyes off her mouth. "You make everything better than expected."

"Not when it comes to baking or cooking." Robin shook her head. "Although I did get lucky this time, even if Winona's prophecies don't always come true."

"What do you mean?" Dylan asked around another mouthful of cookie.

"She made a comment about me winning and losing. I might not have been first, but I also wasn't last. So I guess I neither won nor lost."

"If you ask me," Dylan said as he swallowed his last bite, "I don't know how someone could have voted for anyone else."

Robin narrowed her eyes at him. "I guess I must be an acquired taste."

"I seem to have definitely acquired it," he said, then leaned his head to hers and captured her mouth in a kiss. This time, he wasn't testing the waters with a soft kiss goodbye or staking his claim to her in front of some young pup who had no business making eyes at her.

When Dylan hauled her against him, he was telling her in no uncertain terms that they should have done this a while ago. Robin's fingers slid around his neck and he lowered his hands to draw her hips closer so that she was standing between his open knees. When she opened her lips to moan, he took the opportunity to deepen the kiss with his tongue.

She responded just as eagerly and pressed her body against his.

But the phone ringing out at the reception area reminded him of where he was. He quickly pulled his head back, completely dazed.

Her eyelids were still half-closed, her pink lips swollen and her hands resting gently on his shoulders. Dylan growled before pulling her back for a second, longer kiss. His hands moved to her waist and his thumbs grazed the bare spot between her jeans and her sweater. Robin gasped as he slipped his hands higher, his palms on fire against her silky soft skin. She arched toward him, her hardened nipples grazing his chest, and all he could think about was touching her everywhere. And all at once.

His fingers were at the back clasp of her bra when Robin pulled back suddenly.

Had he done something wrong? Was he taking things too quickly? When he was able to draw a ragged breath he asked. "Are you okay?"

She nodded slowly and whispered, "I'm fine, but I think I heard one of the salespeople out there."

"Oh wow," Dylan said, completely releasing her then dragging his fingers through his hair. "I'm so sorry, Robin. I don't know what's gotten into me. I totally forgot where we were. If you hadn't stopped me, you probably would've ended up on my desk…" He shook his head to clear the steamy image and get himself under control. "Sorry. You deserve better than this."

She placed her palms on either side of his face,

forcing him to meet her eyes. "Listen, Dylan. It's not your fault this happened. It's the cookies."

He blinked several times and then laughed, but she didn't drop her hands.

"I know it sounds ludicrous, but they're from this old family recipe, and legend has it that when measured with the right hands, it's supposed to melt the hardest of hearts. I guess it meant literal hands for measuring and this was the first time I used mine. Or maybe it was when you touched the bag of sugar to pick it up. I don't know, but the recipe has never worked for me before, yet today for some reason, it's working." She bit her adorable lower lip then added, "Maybe a little too well."

His brain was still foggy with passion as he processed her sentences. But his mind couldn't get past one. "You think I have a hard heart?"

"No," she said, using her thumbs to trace along his jawline. "But do you have another explanation for this sudden need to kiss me no matter who's outside that open door?"

He returned his hands to her waist. "It wasn't exactly sudden. I've been thinking about it for a while. I'm a grown man, Robin, and I refuse to believe that some love potion is calling the shots here. I wanted to kiss you. I still want to kiss you."

Robin, who had yet to respond to his most forward advances, finally pulled his face closer to hers and then boldly said, "So what's stopping you?"

## *Chapter Thirteen*

Robin didn't know how they got out of the dealership so quickly without anyone noticing them, but they had. Of course, by the time they'd left, most of the crowd was already gone anyway. Only the party rental company packing up their equipment and Dylan's staff, who he said were working on double commission for the event, remained.

Dylan pulled her through a secret door in the service garage, leading her to the back alley where he'd parked his truck. He gave her another deep kiss as soon as they were safely inside the cab and Robin was floating with excitement. This was what she had wanted that first day she'd walked into the dealership. It was the entire reason she'd entered the bake-off. She'd wanted Dylan to notice her.

When they walked into his empty apartment a

few minutes later, she realized he was about to notice all of her. It wasn't that she was self-conscious of her body. She'd always been athletic and in relatively good shape. It was just that she'd never been fully naked with a man before when it wasn't completely dark outside.

The sun hadn't even set, yet Dylan had her pressed up against the door, his mouth trailing kisses along her throat and his hands making quick work of her sweater.

"Should we close the curtains?" she whispered.

"Probably," he said, but instead of walking across the small living room to do so, he continued to make love to her mouth as he expertly backed her down a hallway and into a bedroom. The vertical blinds on the window were closed, but still allowed for a decent amount of light. Robin once thought she'd be a trembling mass of nerves and anxiety if she'd ever successfully made it this far with Dylan, but her fingers didn't so much as quiver as she steadily undid each of the buttons on his shirt. When she pushed the fabric from his shoulders, she was rewarded with the sight she'd been fantasizing about for weeks. His tan skin was smooth and warm with a scattering of dark hair across his well-defined chest. The ridges of his ab muscles made a perfect pattern as his waist narrowed, the dark hair tapering to a thin trail along his belly button and lower into his pants.

She didn't get enough time to explore him, because as soon as his shirt hit the ground, he was reaching behind her to unclasp her bra. She returned the favor by undoing the fly of his pants. He clasped her hands. "Hold that thought. I have to go grab something."

She quickly shed her jeans and was trying to figure out the sexiest way to position herself on his bed when he returned with an unopened box of condoms. He froze as he seemed to be drinking in the sight of her. For the first time in Robin's life, her body actually hummed with the awareness of her own sexuality.

Leaning back on her elbows, wearing nothing but her panties and a smile, she relished the sound of his exhaled groan as he strode confidently toward her. As she looked up at him expectantly, he said, "You are the most beautiful woman I've ever seen."

And it was so easy to allow herself to believe that.

He set the condoms on the nightstand and finished unzipping his pants. When his arousal sprang free, Robin gulped. Was there anything about this man that wasn't perfect?

He eased himself onto the bed beside her and resumed kissing her slowly, making his way from her lips down to her breasts. When he took one of her aching nipples into his mouth, Robin arched against him, moaning his name. She needed this. She needed him. And she told him so.

"You're sure," he asked.

"Now please," she replied, sliding her panties down her hips as he reached for a foil packet.

When he entered her, he whispered her name and it was the most erotic sound she'd ever heard. She lifted her knees to take him deeper inside and nearly shattered at the intense pleasure of his first full thrust.

She had been trying to play it cool, but there was no way she was going to last. It had been too long and she'd been wanting him so badly. She rocked her hips against him, and the friction was too much for her to bear. Robin threw back her head as waves of pleasure shuddered through her body.

Dylan held himself perfectly still as her inner muscles clenched around him. When her climax was over, she blinked up at him, her lips open as she gasped, her lungs only able to draw in small amounts of air at a time. She panted when she said, "I'm sorry I didn't wait for you."

He grasped her hips and deftly rolled them over so that Robin was on top. His hands slid up to her waist and, as she sat up straighter, he moaned. "There. Now you can make it up to me."

And she did just that.

Dylan watched the woman sleeping beside him and wondered why last night had been so great. He'd slept with plenty of women in the past, but with Robin, it had been different. This time, he hadn't wanted to leave in the morning. Of course, he also didn't usually bring anyone back to his place so it wasn't as though he could make a swift exit. At least not politely.

But with Robin, there was no urgency to get away. No sense that she was going to wake up beside him and expect a ring on her finger. Listening to her breathe as she curled against him, he realized things felt different because this was the first time he'd slept with someone who understood his goals and shared his determination. Someone who was his friend first. Someone who would hopefully be his friend afterward.

When she stirred awake, he kissed her forehead softly.

His bedding was clean, but basic, and his apartment sparsely furnished since Dante had fully moved out. He could only imagine the plush decor of the bedroom where Robin normally slept. But since she still lived on her family's property and the house on his ranch was currently missing a roof, this had been the only place where he could bring her.

She stretched against him as she opened her eyes, taking in her surroundings. If she was disappointed by the inexpensive apartment, she was too polite to say so. Instead, she said, "Those sure were some cookies, huh?"

He laughed, causing her hand to move up and down as his chest vibrated. "They were good, but I'm telling you it wasn't the cookies."

She had to push the hair out of her eyes. "How do you know?"

"Because if they contained any traces of a love potion, it'd clearly be out of my system now. And yet, I still want to do this."

She yelped as he flipped her onto her back, but her giggles soon became moans as his head moved lower to her small, rounded breasts, and then lower still.

Thirty minutes later, he was in the shower and she came padding into the bathroom barefoot and wearing one of his University of Montana T's. "Dylan, I can't find your coffeepot."

"That's because I took it out to the ranch so the construction crew could use it."

"Well, that was thoughtful of you. But then what do you drink in the mornings?"

"I'm usually not home long enough." She hadn't asked, but she'd probably seen the meager supplies in his kitchen as well as the single recliner in the living room. He knew from experience that it would be best to explain now. "This apartment is just a place for me to sleep. A temporary home until the house on the ranch is habitable and I can finally move in."

Although, the truth was that when he said *temporary*, he left off the part where it had been that way for the past several years. But even when he and Dante had signed the original lease, Dylan had known he would end up in a bigger place eventually. He just needed to live somewhere cheap enough while he was saving his money. Once the ranch was done, it still might not be quite as extravagant as Robin was already used to, but it would be his.

"So no coffee. No breakfast." Robin leaned against the bathroom counter. "What do you usually offer the morning after...you know?"

"I guess we're about to find out." He ducked his head back under the water to rinse the shampoo. When he shut off the faucet, he said, "We could go grab some breakfast. The Gemstone Diner has the best hashbrowns in town."

"Dylan, we can't go out in public for a sit-down breakfast the morning after Valentine's Day with me wearing the same clothes I had on yesterday." Robin had left her truck parked back at the dealership and was completely at his mercy. "Everyone will know."

"Know what?" He wiggled his eyebrows. She threw his towel at him but he easily caught it. "Just wear something of mine. I might have some smaller sweat-pants."

"Yeah, everything you own that would fit me has some sort of college or sports logo on it. Pretty sure that would be a dead giveaway, as well."

"Keep staring at me like that and you won't be wearing anything soon," he said as he dried off.

This time she was the one who wiggled her eye-brows. But she didn't take him up on either of his invitations. "I should probably get home and take a shower."

"You took one last night," he reminded her.

"I know and now I smell like…" She picked up the bottle of shower gel sitting on the edge of his tub and read, "'Endurance, Speed and Cedarwood.' Plus, I need to pick up my truck, which is parked right in front of Bronco Motors with the Bonnie B logo right there on the door."

Dylan almost suggested that people would likely think that the truck was getting dropped off for ser-vice. But she was already shooting down every idea he could come up with to get her to hang out longer. Old insecurities he thought he'd overcome long ago threatened to surface again. No. He wasn't going to compare Robin to his ex.

The Abernathys were an established and well-respected family in the community and Robin had more than her own reputation to consider. It was one thing for the gossips to think they were dating. It was another to think that this was… Dylan wasn't exactly sure what this was between them.

"So then how about we hit a drive-through for some coffee and a breakfast sandwich and then go grab your truck?"

Robin nodded. "That works. What time do you plan to be at Broken Road Ranch today?"

"Probably not until the afternoon. I'm going to be buried processing registration tags all morning and running inventory reports. Trust me, it's just as boring as it sounds, but it also means that yesterday's event was a major success."

"Good," she said then rose on her tiptoes to kiss his cheek. "Because people will probably expect another bake-off next year."

"It'll be worth it if you make more of those Heartmelters for me."

"Sadly, I'm retiring my red apron after last night." Robin shook her head. "No more contests for me. They're too stressful."

"Then I'm retiring my microphone duties for the same reason. You'll still make me the cookies, though, right? Like a custom order?"

"I'm not committing to anything until I get some coffee," she said as she walked out of the bathroom and retreated down the hall.

Dylan kissed her goodbye when he dropped her off at her truck and they made plans to meet at his ranch that afternoon. The demo would be done by then and they needed to bring the cows back to the barn before the weather decided to shift gears and dump a few more inches of snow.

When he walked into his office, he whistled at the sales numbers from the previous day, which Mickie had been keeping a tally of on a whiteboard in the break room. He was even more thrilled to see that there were still a few cookies on the plate he'd left on his desk.

As predicted, he was up to his elbows in paper-work and sent Robin a text telling her he might be a little late meeting her at the ranch. She responded that she already had Buttermilk and Maze Runner loaded in the trailer and had enlisted her brother Theo to go with her.

Still, Dylan didn't like the fact that it was yet another job on his property that he wasn't doing himself. Unfortunately, the dealership was the only thing currently keeping the ranch afloat and his attention was also needed there.

It also didn't sit well with him that he was relying on Robin more than he should. What happened if she decided that she was done with this little project of hers? What happened when she was done with him? After the passion-filled night they'd just shared, Dylan wasn't ready to contemplate that. He fired off a text thanking her then added, Dinner tonight?

She didn't respond for a while and he told himself it was because she was driving. Then he told himself it was because the reception might not be the best on the ranch. Although, it had always been decent before. By four o'clock, he'd eaten way too many cookies and had been staring at way too many numbers. He grabbed his coat and headed toward the door. "I'm taking off, Mickie. I'll see you tomorrow."

His office manager was on the phone and waved him off. By the time he got to the ranch, he was amazed to see that the dumpster full of rotted roof shingles had been hauled away and there was a fresh layer of new ones on the roof. Dylan was also relieved to see the cows in the pasture adjacent to the barn and Robin and Theo walking their horses toward the trailer.

"Dylan?" Robin lifted her brows in surprise, but smiled. "I thought you were stuck at the office."

"How's it going, Theo?" he said to her brother.

Theo had a podcast talking about everything ranching, but Dylan was usually too busy listening to sports radio to catch many of the episodes. He should probably start making more of an effort. He might learn something. "Hey, man. I heard Trail Boss here came in second at the bake-off."

"She did. I finished off the rest of the cookies she made before noon."

"Never thought I'd see the day." Theo shook his head then took Maze Runner's reins from his sister's hand and continued on to the trailer. That was an odd response.

Robin walked toward Dylan. "Is something wrong?"

"I texted and you didn't respond."

She patted her back pockets. "I must've left my phone in the truck. Did you need something?"

"Dinner. I was hungry and thought you might be, too."

"I could use a bite," Theo said from inside the trailer. Apparently the window had been open.

Dylan hadn't meant to include her brother, but he certainly owed the guy for helping herd cattle today. "You guys want to do Pastabilities?"

"I was kidding, man," Theo said through the open window. "I would only be a third wheel. And besides, I need to get the horses back. Just give Robin a ride home, okay?"

"Sure," Dylan said.

Robin raised her hand. "I can answer for myself, you guys." Then she asked Dylan, "Can you give me a ride home?"

Dylan did give her a ride home, but not until after midnight. They'd had dinner and then stopped by his apartment again to pick up where they'd left off that morning. He wanted Robin to sleep over again, but Dylan knew it wouldn't be a good look for him to drive her back to the Bonnie B when the entire ranch was awake and everyone was starting their work shifts.

And that's how it went for the next couple of days. They'd meet in the afternoons at the ranch before going to grab dinner and end the night back at his place. The only difference was she wouldn't leave until morning—in her own truck—when Dylan left for the dealership.

It was almost as though they were in a...relationship.

## Chapter Fourteen

"Why couldn't Robin make it?" Dylan's mom asked on Sunday evening as the Sanchez family gathered around the dining room at Sofia and Boone's house. His parents' kitchen remodel had finally been completed, but they'd already donated their old dining room table only to find out that the new one couldn't be delivered until tomorrow. Besides, they'd had dinner at Dylan's ranch last week and suddenly all the siblings wanted to take a turn hosting.

"I couldn't very well invite her to dinner at someone else's house," Dylan said.

There was a collective chorus of boos and at least two people muttered, "Give me a break."

His brother-in-law Boone said, "Don't be ridiculous. You know you can invite anyone you want over here."

Dylan tried to change the subject and asked Boone how his brother Shep was doing after their mom told everyone at the bake-off that her son was still single.

"He's probably feeling the exact same way you were at the mayor's anniversary party. You know, when you were getting grumpy about being the only single Sanchez at the table?"

"I wasn't grumpy." Dylan took a scoop of roasted red potatoes. "I was annoyed that I didn't have any elbow room."

"And do you have plenty of elbow room in your apartment when Robin stays the night?" Camilla asked.

He gave his sister a look of warning as he subtly jerked his chin toward their parents.

"Mom and Dad already know," Dante said, not very helpfully.

Their mom took a large gulp of wine then added, "So do all my clients who come into the salon. I'm not sure which topic is gossiped about more—Penny Smith's missing necklace or you and Robin Abernathy."

"What do you expect, Dylan?" Felix said. "How many people have a blue truck with the Bonnie B logo stenciled on the side that they park in front of your apartment?"

"At least twelve since her family just bought a few from Bronco Motors to add to their fleet. How do they know that truck doesn't belong to one of the ranch foremen?"

"Does it?" The question came from his brother-in-law Jordan.

"You know it doesn't," Dylan muttered. Then he cleared his throat. "I don't remember you guys talking about Eloise's car being parked in the same spot back when she and Dante started dating."

Eloise passed him the bowl of salad. "Actually, I'm pretty sure everyone in town did."

"Not that I was judging," Dylan said quickly. "I saw no problem with where you parked."

"I'd be careful if I were you, Dylan," Shari said. "Don't forget that Eloise and I are the ones deciding which one of our bridesmaids you're going to be walking down the aisle with."

Dylan's gut dropped.

"Have I told you about Drunk Patty, my roommate from boarding school?" Eloise asked a bit too sweetly.

"I thought Robin was one of your bridesmaids," Dylan's tone was almost accusatory. "Why can't I walk with her?"

And that's when everyone at the table started laughing. Camilla pointed her finger. "See, I knew it."

"Knew what?"

"That things were getting serious between you and Robin."

"No, they're not." Dylan helped himself to two pieces of chicken. "As far as I know, it's a casual relationship."

"Would Robin define it as casual?" his mother asked.

"I don't know because we haven't discussed it. I don't even think we've used the word *relationship* at this point."

"Don't you think you should ask her how she feels?" Dante asked.

"Maybe. Probably." Then Dylan shook his head at his brother. "Don't give me that look like you're some sort of expert at love. You met Eloise a few months before I met Robin."

"You know what you need?" Sofia tried to pass the salad back to him since he hadn't put any on his plate the first time around. "A grand gesture."

"Yes!" Camilla clapped her hands. "Something big that shows Robin exactly how you feel."

"Last time I let you guys plan a grand gesture for me, I ended up with over two hundred people and a news crew at my dealership."

"And generated a whole lot of sales from it." Jordan took the salad bowl from him. "At least that's what Mickie told her sister when she stopped by my office."

"It's not going to happen," Dylan said firmly to his family. There was no way he was going to put his heart out there only to get rejected again. Especially not publicly.

"If that's the case," his father said, chiming in for the first time, "if it *really* is only a casual relationship, then you should probably end it now before someone starts falling in love."

His father's words felt like a swift kick in the stomach. But with everyone voicing their disagreement, Dylan's head throbbed as though it had also been kicked.

"That's the worst advice I've ever heard, Dad," Camilla said, and Sofia nodded emphatically. But

Dylan had completely lost his appetite and was tuning out the conversation.

"Excuse me, I'll be right back," he said to nobody in particular and stood to use the restroom.

But he kept on walking right out the front door.

Because he didn't want them to worry about him—or bug him—Dylan sent a text in the family group chat saying something came up and he'd talk to them tomorrow. Then he drove home with his dad's words echoing in his brain. Maybe his father was right. Dylan didn't want to be the one who fell in love only to have Robin end things. And the way things were going now, he was certainly at risk of doing exactly that.

Robin had once suggested that Dylan didn't put his foot down very often. But when it came to his heart, he had to draw a line somewhere. The longer he let things go on, the worse it was going to get.

He needed to ask her if he stood a chance.

Robin tried not to think about the fact that she had spent nearly every day with Dylan for the past two weeks. And yet, when Sunday rolled around, he hadn't said a word about bringing her with him to his family's weekly dinner. The only reason she'd dined with them last week was because they'd shown up on the ranch unannounced.

Was this Dylan's way of letting her know that things weren't serious between them? She could help him on his ranch. She could split the appetizer sampler platter with him at Doug's bar as she'd done last night. She could sleep in his bed. But she wasn't good enough to take home to his family.

It stung.

Yet, she would give him whatever space he needed. They hadn't defined their relationship, so if she'd been misreading the situation and expecting something he wasn't ready to give, then she only had herself to blame. The man had a reputation for a reason. He'd never pretended to be anything else.

Robin decided to distract herself by catching up on some emails and supply orders she needed to make. Up until now, she'd been outsourcing production of her braces and magnetic blankets to a manufacturing company in Kalispell. But maybe she should start looking into investing in a factory for Rein Rejuvenation here in Bronco.

When her phone rang at nine o'clock and she saw Dylan's name on the screen, she sighed a breath of relief—he hadn't forgotten about her—and then steeled her jaw in annoyance at the thought that he better not expect her to come running over now that he was available. She waited until the fourth ring to answer.

"Hey, Robin. How are you?"

This wasn't a good sign. He never began calls that way. At least not with her. Usually, he didn't waste time and launched straight into a familiar topic. "I'm fine. How are you?"

"I'm okay. I think." Yep, something was wrong. She was accustomed to him being way more chatty.

Robin's own nerves were already raw. Perhaps taking control of the conversation would help ground her. "Something on your mind, Dylan?"

"Actually, a lot is. I don't know where to start."

"This might be a first," Robin said, cringing at the cattiness in her tone. But sometimes you had to take the bull by the horns before it could knock you to the ground. "Dylan Sanchez, the smooth-talking salesman who always knows just what to say, suddenly doesn't know where to start."

"That's fair, I guess," he replied. "I wasn't even sure I could make this phone call, but I knew it would be worse if I didn't."

She clenched the phone harder in her hand and bit her trembling lip. This was it. He was about to break her heart. If there was any time to take control of a situation, this was it. She'd save them both the trouble.

"Look, Dylan, I think we both know that we were never meant to be together long term. You needed someone to help you on your ranch and I needed a project. It was fun while it lasted. Don't worry about it."

"Wow," was all he said before a long, excruciating pause. She could hear him take a ragged breath, which only made her heart ache more. Was he relieved that she'd made it so easy? He finally continued, "You seem to be totally fine with this."

"How else should I be?" she countered. It wasn't exactly like she had a choice. If the man wanted to call things off with her, she couldn't very well cry and beg him to stay. Not when she knew that deep down, he didn't want her. "Listen, I'm in the middle of researching some stuff for work so if we're good here, I need to wrap this up."

Her voice shook with the last two words because she also needed to wrap herself up in a giant blanket and have a good cry.

"Um, yeah. I guess we're good, then. Take care, Rob—"

"You, too," she cut him off, knowing she couldn't bear to hear her name on his lips. "Bye."

Robin disconnected the phone, ran a hot bath and then soaked all night in her tears.

She'd barely slept and was especially cranky the following morning when she went out to the stables and saw her brother Jace pointing out the horses to his son, Frankie. Her brother must have the day off from working at the fire station and wanted to let Tamara sleep in.

With everyone around her getting married and having babies, Robin felt as though she was falling behind and, at this rate, would never catch up. She almost went down the opposite row of stables to avoid the reminder that she was still alone. But at the last minute she decided she could use a happy distraction.

"There's my favorite seven-month-old," she cooed to her nephew as she approached.

"What's wrong with your eyes?" Jace shifted his baby to his other hip, farther away from her. "Do you have an infection or something?"

Robin did feel as though she was squinting more this morning. "Not that I know of. Why?"

"They're all red and swollen, like you're having an allergic reaction."

She sighed. "Yeah, it's called an allergic reaction to love."

"Wait." Jace's face filled with concern. "You were crying? But the Trail Boss never cries."

"Well, I guess there's a first time for everything."

"Was it Dylan?" Jace frowned. "Do I need to go have a talk with him?"

Robin rarely gave her brothers the opportunity to be protective over her since she usually handled everything herself. But it made her feel better to know that her family had her back.

Robin forced a smile but shook her head. "Remember that time when I was about twelve or so and we were out riding and came across that wild mustang with the injured hoof?"

"Yeah, I remember it took you about two hours to get it to trust you enough to get close. And then another three to slowly walk it back to the stables. You made that soft boot for it out of your favorite sweatshirt and nursed it back to health. I'm pretty sure that was when you first got the idea that you could make custom therapeutic devices for horses."

"It was. But it was also the first time I learned that just because I put enough energy into something and try to tame it, some animals are just meant to be free."

Frankie made a gurgling sound and Jace looked at his son. "Yeah, I'm confused, too, buddy. But I think Dylan is supposed to be the wild mustang in this analogy."

Robin would have rolled her eyes at her brother, but her lids were too swollen from crying to make it effective. "More than anything, I'm mad at myself for believing things with him could have ended any other way."

Jace's expression became more serious. "Who says it ended?"

"I did. Last night when he called me, I could tell in his voice that something was wrong. So I cut my losses."

"That might've been a bit premature, sis. I seriously doubt you and Dylan are done. There's too much heat between the two of you."

"What are you talking about?"

"More like what everyone in town is talking about. I only saw you guys together once at the bake-off."

"We weren't together. He was busy networking and selling cars."

"And you were too busy making those cookies that you couldn't see the way he rarely took his eyes off you all afternoon."

A seed of hope took root in her chest, but she wasn't about to let it blossom. "No, Dylan looks that way at everyone."

"Not at Bethany McCreery or that Gabrielle woman who's new to town. And definitely not at Mr. Brandt."

She didn't want to tell her brother that Dylan's interest was likely only due to the Heartmelters and the love potion effect they'd had on him. Although, he hadn't eaten any cookies until *after* the contest... Nope. Robin wasn't going to even consider it.

"Come on, Jace. You know as well as I do that the

Sanchez brothers have a reputation for their charm and their flirtatious smiles."

"And now two of them are about to get married," Jace said. "So maybe their reputations should have been that they just hadn't found the right women yet."

"When has any man ever thought of me as the right woman?" Robin asked. "I've always been one of the guys."

"Or have you always acted like one of the guys just to fit in? You live on a ranch surrounded by cowboys. The men who want to earn their paychecks know better than to look at you the way Dylan Sanchez does."

Robin tried not to be swayed by Jace's assessment. She also tried not to be swayed by Brad's group text to her and Dylan later that morning about the height of the bathroom tiles. She wasn't going to respond because the Broken Road Ranch was no longer her concern. If she was going to survive this breakup, then she needed a clean break. She wasn't going to so much as think about the man.

And she didn't. Until Eloise stopped by the Bonnie B later in the week to show Robin some preliminary designs for Rein Rejuvenation's European marketing campaign.

Without any prompting by Robin, her friend blurted out, "So Dylan was a mess at the Sanchez family dinner last Sunday."

"Maybe his mind was preoccupied with replenishing the stock of vehicles that seem to be flying off his lot since the bake-off." Not that Robin had purposely driven by the dealership in the hopes of catching a glimpse of him. Because that would've been stalker-ish. Although, on Tuesday, she'd had an unexpected craving for a double bacon cheeseburger from Bronco Burgers and had inadvertently driven past there. But that was by accident and she went completely out of her way to take a different route home.

"He didn't even make it through dinner, Robin. He took off during the middle of the meal and left a plate full of food behind. And you know that guy never leaves food behind. Oh, and did I mention that he left right after I threatened to have him walk down the aisle at my wedding with my boarding school room-mate Drunk Patty?"

"I met your former roommate in Rust Creek Falls when we were trying on bridesmaid dresses. She was lovely and very sober. Why would Dylan leave over that?"

"Because he wants *you*, Robin."

"That's not the impression he gave me on Sunday night when he called to end things."

Eloise gasped. "Oh no. I'm afraid his dad made a suggestion that evening and Dylan misinterpreted it. Did he really call to end things?"

"Well, he called. I was the one who had to end it."

"Just so I'm clear, he didn't actually break up with you?" Eloise asked. "Or tell you that he didn't want to see you anymore?"

"Not exactly." Robin flipped through the pages of Eloise's portfolio, refusing to glance up and risk hav-ing her friend give her any sort of sign of false hope. "But if he wants to see me, he knows where to find me. Besides, I already made the first move by going out of my comfort zone and entering that bake-off contest. It's his turn now."

"Good to know," Eloise said, then flipped the portfolio around so it was right side up and started talking about the ad images.

The fact that Robin had spoken those soul-crushing words so easily, so casually, only made Dylan feel more miserable. Before he could find the right words to ask her where they stood, she'd acted as though she were doing them both a favor. Proving that she hadn't seen their relationship as anything more than a good time.

And that had been what hurt the most.

Dylan looked up from the stack of hay bales he was hauling into the barn and saw his father's mail truck pulling into his driveway. He glanced down at his watch as his dad walked over. "Running a little late on your route today, huh, Dad?"

Normally, Aaron Sanchez delivered to this side of town in the morning and Dylan didn't get a chance to see him since he was only at the ranch later in the afternoons.

"I decided to switch things up today." His dad scanned the area where the construction crew was parked. "I haven't seen Robin's truck out here the past few mornings and thought I'd swing by and see if something happened."

"Yeah, something happened, Dad. I did what you said and called her to have the talk and…well, we broke up." No need to tell his father that Dylan hadn't been the one who'd officially said the words.

His dad smacked himself in the forehead and muttered a string of curses in Spanish. Then switched back to English as though his son hadn't been able to understand the bad words. "You were supposed to do the *opposite* of that, Dylan."

Dylan's eyebrows slammed together. "So you *didn't* want me to take your advice?"

"Of course not. Why would I want you to break up with Robin? She's the best thing that ever happened to you."

Closing his eyes, Dylan tried to take a steadying breath. "Then why would you tell me to call things off before someone got their heart broken?"

"Because, son, the thought of losing Robin was supposed to force you to make the right decision. It was reverse psychology."

Dylan groaned. "Then why didn't you just tell me how much my life would suck without her?"

It had only been a few days since he'd last spoken to Robin and he'd hated every single one of them. He missed her smile. He missed her bossiness. He missed the way she fit so perfectly tucked up against his side. He couldn't stop thinking of her. Or of ways to convince her to give him another chance.

"Look, Dylan. You've always been the type of person who wants more for himself. You were like that when you played T-ball, yet insisted on being the team pitcher. You were like that during high school when you bought that lifted 4x4 that looked cool but had a salvaged title and barely ran. You were certainly like that well before you ever met what's-her-name in college."

Dylan froze. He'd never told anyone in his family about his ex-girlfriend. "How did you know about Maribel?"

"Well, I didn't know for sure until right this minute. All I knew was that you were home for a visit, and I was on the side of the house trying to find a basketball Dante had overshot when a young gal pulled up to the house in a sleek, black convertible with a University of Montana bumper sticker."

He remembered that car well. It was flashy and expensive, just like its owner. It represented everything Dylan had thought he wanted in life.

"Back then," his dad continued, "it was no big deal for you kids to invite friends over for dinner. But that girl stared at our house for several long moments—as if trying to decide whether or not she should come inside—before finally driving away."

Dylan shoved his hands in his pockets and rocked back on his heels. He'd never been ashamed of his parents' modest home, but he was ashamed that he'd almost subjected his family to such a horrible snob.

"I'd been planning on introducing her to you guys that day. But she never showed." What he didn't tell his dad was that he returned that night to his dorm to find a letter under his door.

Maribel had written that she tried, but she just couldn't be with someone who came from such a different background. She needed to be with a guy who was "going places and could afford the type of lifestyle" she expected. Dylan had been devastated. But looking back, it was nothing compared to how his world had come crashing down when Robin told him it was fun while it lasted.

"I noticed a shift in your attitude right after that girl drove away," his dad said. "You switched majors from sports medicine to business and all of sudden, every time you came home for a visit, all you could talk about was being successful and making money."

Being dumped like that had been the driving force behind Dylan's desire to become whatever it was Maribel thought he couldn't be. He was proud of his roots and proud of being from Bronco, and he'd be damned if he was going to let some spoiled daddy's girl tell him he couldn't achieve financial success.

As if reading his mind, his father clapped a hand on his shoulder and said, "Surely, you've learned by now that success isn't measured by wealth or even skill. It's measured by happiness."

"Maybe that's the kind of advice you should give me next time, Dad, instead of the reverse psychology." Dylan leaned into his father's one-arm hug. "Not that I'm blaming you. Obviously, it was my pride that caused me to let the happiest thing in my life slip away because I was too afraid of taking a chance."

"You didn't think Robin would be like your ex, did you?" His dad made a tsking sound. "I mean, if the girl didn't take off running when she saw the condition of this place, then she clearly wanted to be with you because of who you are and not what you own. At least she *did* before you blew it."

"Thanks for the pep talk." Dylan didn't bother hiding his sarcasm. "Now, do you have any *helpful* words of wisdom for how I should win her back?"

Aaron Sanchez smiled, his knowing grin revealing the same dimples Dylan had inherited. "It just so happens that your mom and your sisters have an idea for a grand gesture."

## *Chapter Fifteen*

The last thing Robin wanted to do was attend the Heritage Rodeo at the Bronco Convention Center the last week of February. But Eloise had convinced her that with rodeo superstar Geoff Burris making his last appearance in the States before leaving for Europe with his fiancée, Stephanie Brandt, it would be a great opportunity for Rein Rejuvenation to get some exposure as a sponsor before launching its overseas ad campaign.

"I still don't know why I need to be here in person, though," Robin grumbled as she, Eloise and Stacy found their seats in the stands.

Stacy fluffed Robin's hair. "Because when they announce your company as a sponsor, it'd be nice for them to have a face to associate with the brand."

"I don't want to be on camera, though, Eloise,"

Robin told her friend. "You told the rodeo producers that, right?"

Except Eloise was talking to Dr. and Mrs. Burris, who were here to cheer on their sons, Geoff, Jack and Ross, who were all participating tonight.

"Here, put on some of my lipstick." Stacy already had the tube inches from Robin's face. Unless she wanted to risk looking like one of the rodeo clowns, she better hold still.

"I bet you're going to miss Geoff and Stephanie when they go to Europe," someone said to the Burrises from the row behind them. It was Deborah Dalton.

"We will," Jeanne Burris replied. "We're used to the kids doing so much traveling already on the rodeo circuit, but that doesn't make it any easier when they're gone. We're just lucky that Ross was able to be home in time for the event."

"Now tell me, is Ross still single?" Mrs. Dalton asked, and when Mrs. Burris nodded, she continued, "Because you know my Shep still hasn't settled down yet, either. I'd just really love for him to find a nice girl..."

"Maybe we should find somewhere else to sit," Robin whispered to her sister.

Stacy's face paled. "We can't. I mean, why would you want to do that?"

"Because we're both single and if you haven't noticed, Mrs. Dalton is right behind us and eager to play matchmaker."

The music stopped long enough for the announcer to welcome everyone, and Robin tried not to fidget in her seat as she remembered the last time she was in this building. She'd been convincing Birdsey Jones that she and Dylan were a couple so that he wouldn't bid on the bull Dylan wanted. Or rather the bull Robin had wanted for him. She almost reached for her phone to text Dylan and ask him if the sire had been delivered as scheduled.

In fact, this past week, she'd found herself doing the same thing. Thinking about something that needed to be done on Broken Road Ranch and then stopping herself before she reached out to him to ask. Although, when she ran into Manuel out at the Bonnie B, she'd asked the foreman if his nephew had ever met with Dylan. She'd found out that he had and, starting next week, Dylan would have someone else working with him out at the ranch and wouldn't need her help.

A familiar empty ache settled in her chest and she had to remind herself to stop thinking of him and focus on the rodeo.

The barrel racing was first, which Robin always enjoyed since it had also been her specialty when she'd competed. Right after the last contestant rode out, her brother Theo walked up the steps past their aisle and winked at Stacy, who was sitting on the end.

"Why did Theo just wink at you?" Robin asked.

"I don't think it was at me. Maybe it was someone behind us. Hey, do you mind if we switch seats so I can talk to Eloise about something real quick?"

Robin didn't see why Stacy couldn't just lean forward and talk around her, but she stood. "Sure. I'm going to go get a drink anyway."

Stacy grabbed her arm and pulled her back down. "You can't leave yet."

"Why not? The barrel racing is over, and the break-away roping won't start for a few more minutes."

"Because…" Stacy's eyes seemed to be searching for something in the distance. When the lights in the arena dimmed, she said, "Because it'll be too dark for you to see. Just wait until they announce…whatever they're going to announce."

Except it wasn't an announcement. The jumbotron suddenly lit up with the words "Bronco Motors Car Deals for Cowboys."

Great, now Robin was going to have to sit here and watch a commercial for Dylan's dealership because she couldn't very well get up to leave and risk having people think she was affected by the reminder of him.

Which she was. Her throat was already constricting.

When a spotlight shined into the arena entrance, though, something told her it was going to be much worse than a commercial. Suddenly, she saw Dylan himself and he was decked out in Western garb— including the hat she'd picked out for him at the live-stock auction—and riding in a horse.

Robin's jaw fell open and she nearly slid out of her seat. What in the world was the man doing? He hated being the center of attention and yet here he was on a ridiculously big jumbotron in front of thousands of people doing some rendition of the cheesy car sales-man commercial.

"You might've heard of Bronco Motors, home of

the famous Valentine's Day Bake-Off." His smooth voice came through the speakers. "That's right, ladies and gentlemen, Bronco Motors is a one-stop shop for finding quality cars and quality baked goods."

"Hurry, let me talk to Eloise," Stacy whispered, trying to switch places again, but Robin was glued to her seat, her eyes in wide-open shock as she watched the live train wreck of a commercial taking place in front of her.

Had he lost a bet? She tried to tell herself that she shouldn't care. But as painful as it was to see him so soon after their break-up, it was even more heart-wrenching to see someone she still cared about make a complete fool out of himself.

"We've got great deals every day of the week," he continued. "But tonight's special offer is a once-in-a-lifetime opportunity for just one lucky recipient in the stands."

Several spotlights weaved throughout the crowd as though searching for a person to land on. When the drumroll stopped, the light was directly over their area and Stacy's face was on the jumbotron screen.

Her sister squeaked and then pointed at Robin and yelled, "Not me. Her."

The camera pivoted to Robin and suddenly, it was her face with all of its slack-jawed confusion filling the screen.

"Smile." Eloise elbowed her as the crowd cheered. "Try to look natural."

Natural? Robin was naturally mortified. And possibly paralyzed with uncertainty. Yet, Dylan kept speaking. "Robin, you once made me an offer that you'd teach me something if I was willing to learn. Well, you held your end of the bargain and these past weeks I learned that I could actually feel the kind of love that I feel when I'm with you."

Nope, she wasn't paralyzed. Every nerve ending inside her body began tingling with anticipation as the audience broke out into oohs and awws when Dylan dismounted…was that Buttermilk? That was her horse. From the Bonnie B. That meant her family…

"Were you in on this?" Robin said as her head whipped to Stacy, only to find her sister standing with both their and Dylan's family a few steps behind her.

Eloise nudged her again and Robin turned back around in time to see Dylan coming up the steps toward her. She alternated between confusion and euphoria and the earlier tingling sensation was now generating enough warmth from inside her core that she was sure the radiating glow surrounding her was coming from inside her body and not the spotlight still shining on her. "It was you, and not your cookies, that melted this icy heart of mine, and I will never be the same. I love you, Robin Abernathy, and now I'm the one with a once-in-a-lifetime offer to make you."

Robin, needing to regain some sense of control, stood up, but her knees nearly gave out. Was this really happening?

When he was directly in front of her, she finally found her voice and asked, "What kind of offer? Because I already have a car."

"The kind of offer that involves this…" Dylan

reached into his front shirt pocket and dropped down to one knee.

The crowd roared and nearly drowned out his voice as he opened a jewelry box that displayed a...key.

"Since we do so well picking out stuff together, I wanted to wait until you said yes before we go ring shopping. But this is for the front door at the Broken Road Ranch and represents all of my dreams that I want to keep sharing with you. I know you have plenty more to teach me and if you're willing, Robin, I'm ready to keep learning. What you see is what you get with me, but I will always try my best to be a man worthy of you. That is, if *you* want me. I can be pretty stubborn sometimes. I can—"

Robin put a finger on his lips. "Save the sales pitch and just kiss me."

The applause was nearly deafening when he stood and she flung herself into his arms, his mouth quickly claiming hers. When he pulled away, he held her face in his hands. "I'm sorry for not believing in you. For not believing in us. I was trying to save myself from getting my heart broken only to find out that it would hurt worse to not have you in my life."

Robin thought her chest was going to explode with how much love she felt for this man who hated making a scene and was currently embracing her on the biggest televised screen in Bronco.

"I'm sorry for jumping to conclusions and not sharing my feelings with you from the beginning," she told him. "I'd also say I'm sorry for pushing myself into your life by signing up for a baking contest I had no business entering and no shot of winning. But if I hadn't walked into your dealership that day, I'd have found some other way to get you to notice me."

"Oh, I'd have noticed you… Wait…" He paused, a crease forming between his brows. "You mean you don't bake?"

Robin shook her head, not the least bit apologetic. "Nope. Does that mean you want to renegotiate your original offer?"

"Not a chance." He smiled and just like the first time Robin laid eyes on those dimples, she was lost.

"I love you, Dylan Sanchez, and I accept your offer for this once-in-a-lifetime opportunity."

"Good because while I was wasting a whole week without you, Brad was finishing our future master bathroom, and all I could think of was getting you out to the ranch so we could christen that new tub—"

Robin slapped her hand over his lapel and threw back her head in laughter. "Your mic is still on, cowboy."

"Then that's our cue to get out of here and go home." He kissed her again and then scooped her up into his arms.

Home. Robin couldn't wait to continue building theirs together.

\* \* \* \* \*

*Look for the next installment in the new continuity*
*Montana Mavericks: The Anniversary Gift*

Maverick's Secret Daughter
*by Catherine Mann*

*On sale March 2024,*
*wherever Harlequin books*
*and ebooks are sold.*